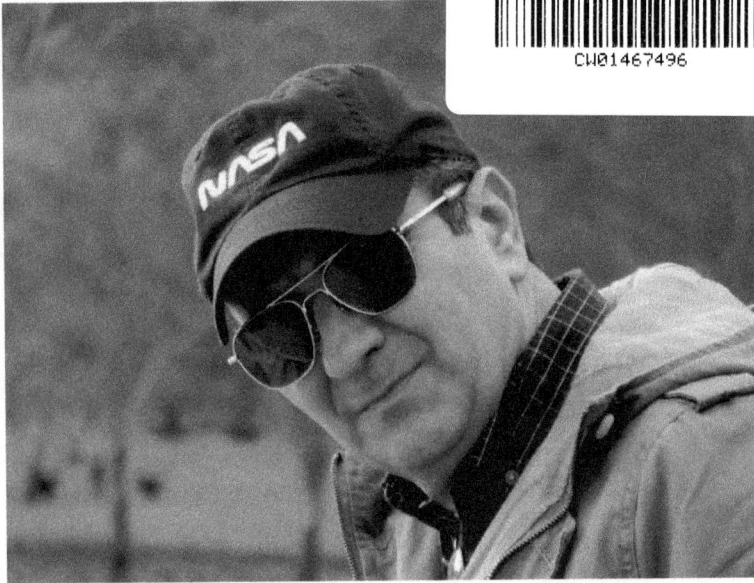

About the Author

Jack Huddson was a crew member of large jets, which allowed him to accumulate a long professional and life experience, but now he is retired. Jack has dedicated his time to writing books since 2005 and several registered manuscripts, Jack's characteristic is that he is a good storyteller, and his next book will be "Far Beyond Borders" full of action, adventures and new characters.

The Mercenary

Jack Huddson

The Mercenary

Olympia Publishers
London

www.olympiapublishers.com
OLYMPIA PAPERBACK EDITION

A CIP catalogue record for this title is
available from the British Library.

ISBN: 978-1-80074-656-5

First Published in 2022

Olympia Publishers
Tallis House
2 Tallis Street
London
EC4Y 0AB
Printed in Great Britain

Dedication

I dedicate this book to my family, who always encouraged me to write and publish my manuscripts, especially to my wife, as my first reader and my daughter, who helped me in many moments with opinions and constructive criticism.

Chapter 1.

That morning the fine rain persisted as I read the news from Le Figaro newspaper at the Café de Flores in Paris, France. The Boulevard Saint-Germain was busy despite the cold weather. I asked the waiter for a cappuccino when I saw Jean-Pierre on the pavement in front of me, with his typical, unmistakable suspicious look. Between his lips, a cigarette insisted on remaining lit, until he took it out of his mouth and dropped it on the street, without any concern. I hadn't seen him for many years. Everyone called him Belgian. The nickname made him proud, despite having a French brother, son of the same father, a product of wanderings and amorous adventures. Jean-Batiste was from Marseille, France. Besides their father, the dark life was a common trait for both of them; some said it was the inheritance their father left them, as their progenitor was a regular visitor to the prisons and with an endless list of transgressions.

My friend Jean-Pierre entered the café by mere chance that only fate explains, as I was not expecting him. He sat down on the opposite side of the large café and after a few minutes was served by the waiter. His clothes were simple and his beard was unshaven a few days ago. That man I met at other times demonstrated the loyalty that few men have experienced. The fine rain intensified showing an almost melancholy day. He ordered coffee and croissant with butter since that was the order served by the waiter. What caught my attention most was his appearance; not that I would judge a person by their attire, but it showed personal carelessness. He knew that the people in the café were watching him with humiliating looks. I didn't understand why, I didn't understand how I had come to that condition of life.

The waiter knew me. He kindly left on the table the hot cappuccino, as well as a glass with water. The Belgian looked hungry. I did not dare to go to him. It seemed to me that simple meal, if it could be called that, brought him to life and I saw him smile at the waiter as he passed by. The fine rain wished to leave the Paris landscape that morning, however, the cold would take a few days.

He was counting the coins on the table to pay the bill, yet I let him follow his own destiny. Jean-Pierre when he met me knew that I had abandoned the humanity that each one carries within, but because of imposed circumstances and not of one's own will. I left the Café de Flores before him and headed for a scheduled business appointment. The Belgian brought back memories of a past kept under lock and key and full of unforgettable and unique adventures.

I was young when I was in Africa for the first time and adult enough to make my own decisions to the point of understanding the magnitude of opportunities the world was showing. Residing in my adventurous soul was the ambition not to be one more in the crowd.

I arrived in Luanda, Angola, at a time of war and terror, a harrowing and cruel civil war. I was a commercial jet pilot. The mission on Angolan soil was to supply the areas with cargo and transport people, civilian or military, wounded and dead. As well as offering maintenance support to the aircraft, since many young people were involved in the frontline battle; and for that "patriotic mission" there was no age, but an AK-47 assault rifle in the name of freedom, and on the other side men willing to take power from their own brothers.

One Saturday afternoon I was informed that a B707 freighter, with no identifying flag and no declared registration plate, was in emergency and would attempt to land. Emergencies were an operational routine for me because, besides the conditions imposed by the civil war, the lack of spare parts and material made those situations constant.

The other pilots and I took off ready for any emergency, and this made us, in a way, experienced and fearless to the point of feeling invulnerability in the blood, something very dangerous for an aviator.

The emergency B707 spiralled down and away from the head of the designated runway until it entered a long final stretch for landing. The pilot appeared experienced keeping the aircraft stable, without flapping the four-engine wings and in the correct attitude, yet the B707 was below the descent ramp; few would dare such irresponsibility, which indicated two possibilities: firstly, a pilot without operational standards; secondly a pilot looking for an accident. The trail of black smoke from the four engines was the unmistakable signature of that magnificent aircraft, of unique beauty and elegance.

The four-engine plane crossed the threshold and landed on the exact mark demonstrating the skill of the pilot-in-command, who elegantly lifted the nose and touched down gently on the runway with the Main Landing Gear, leaving behind the momentary and characteristic smoke from the friction of the tyres with the ground, and immediately positioned the Nose Gear on the runway and commanded the respective and powerful forward and aft thrusters with enthusiasm, however, engine number three stalled abruptly, accompanied by a loud bang. The pilot-in-command undid the reverser in an attempt to avoid engine damage. He let the B707 decelerate masterfully down what remained of the runway.

The aircraft parked, away from the maintenance hangars, while I followed all the movements, including the emergency ground support and nothing beyond the normal daily routine. However, one of the mechanics' assistants approached me to inform me that the B707 crew needed technical support with experience in hydraulic systems. The breakdown was probably a loss of hydraulic fluid, nothing serious, but in-flight procedures must be well handled by the pilots. At that moment two Mig-21 fighter planes tore through the sky on formation less than one thousand five hundred feet above the ground.

Two African mechanics were always with me, and we drove in a car to the aircraft, which mysteriously kept the doors closed, with the engines switched off and without any lighting; however, I knew that in order to help, they should request an AC source of electricity, but in that country, everything has a price, especially for an aircraft without registration plates and flags. After five minutes parked so that the captain could spot me, the flight engineer came down the access known as 41. He was a man of medium height, light blue eyes and red hair; appearing to be Irish.

The supposed Irishman was wearing a khaki shirt and shorts. The shoulder pads confirmed his position in the cockpit. He stared at me and asked in an Irish drawl if I was maintenance. He then asked if I was the boss. I later learned the reason for the question. I did not answer, however, I asked if I wanted an external power plant; he stated yes and I remained quiet waiting. Then the flight engineer understood that nothing was for free and then agreed on a fair price. A frank smile from that Irish face was the first step to a business deal.

I wasted no time. I ordered the mechanics to bring in the external power plant, which they did, while I watched the flight engineer inspect the landing gear, tyres and the number three engine inlet. Soon afterwards he asked for twenty-six cans of hydraulic oil, due to the loss of fluid from the auxiliary hydraulic system. Again, we agreed on a price for the repair service and all material.

The Irishman followed our work and was satisfied. Before finishing, I asked him to open the aircraft's main door; he was suspicious, but agreed, as he knew that some cockpit procedures had to be carried out, and before authorising me, he went to talk to the captain, and after a few minutes the main door was opened by the Irishman.

I climbed aboard alone and when I entered the cockpit I met the flight captain for the first time. His name was Jean-Pierre, and next to him, in the co-pilot position, was his brother, Jean-Batiste. I realised the possibility that the crew was a Tower of Babel.

I have a gift: by looking at a person I can determine their character. When my gaze reached them, I knew that despite their different faces, they had the same look of criminals. Their greeting in French with different accents was clear. I asked Commander Jean-Pierre to rise from the armchair; he examined me with his green eyes from top to bottom several times; he looked at his brother and smiled debauchedly and yielded the armchair while the Irishman brought him a cup of hot coffee in full view. I sat in the left-hand seat and began some procedures; Jean-Batiste was helping me with the hydraulics, when the captain made a derogatory and, once again, debauched comment, which I have never forgotten: "He looks like a pilot."

At that moment I did not hesitate to answer and said: "I'm

currently a B707 and B737-200 Adv pilot, flight engineer and mechanic." Then I stared at him with a look I hadn't expected and said bluntly: "His final was totally below the descent ramp, something very dangerous, but brave." Silence took over the cockpit and not another word was said.

In addition to the hydraulics, the front and rear reversers of the number three engine were repaired. The B707 needed to be refuelled with aviation paraffin and payment was made in cash from a suitcase containing a tidy sum. From the same briefcase came one thousand US dollars for me, plus five hundred dollars for each mechanic and payment for maintenance support material. I finally provided an LPU – Low-Pressure Unit – for the pneumatic starting of the engines.

Before they closed the main door, Commander Jean-Pierre came up to me, in the section between the galley and the main cargo hold, to thank me and extended his right hand in greeting. I accepted it as a gesture of recognition, but as I turned my body to leave the aircraft, he took hold of my right arm and said: "I'm quite sure the chap I work for will be pleased to meet you. He pays well and is looking for capable, efficient and brave pilots."

I looked into Commander Jean-Pierre's eyes. He realised that he had come across someone different and looked away, perhaps out of recklessness. He was not wrong. Without asking he handed me a card containing the name of a company, address and telephone numbers, not without first writing "*Mister Iranian*" on the back. I read it carefully and once again looked into his eyes and thanked him in French, turned around and went down the stairs; then the main door was closed, the stairs removed and the four engines started.

I walked away with the other two mechanics. Commander Jean-Pierre made a perfect taxi to the opposite landing head, lined up the four-engine plane, ran it down the runway and with determination raised the nose of the B707 soaring splendidly into the clouds to the left of the airport. I paid the mechanics what was agreed, and each one handed me fifty dollars of the payment he had handed over, plus one hundred US dollars of my own to pay the airport administrator. Everything has a price, including the ten per cent "fee".

The days passed at different speeds. I had the respect of my commanders and those who participated in some way in the lives of each of us. The two mechanics were from Zaire, experienced and loyal, as well as being very good cooks. The eldest was "Babu", which means: "Being the tenth son", the other was "Akin", which means: "Brave warrior".

Life in Africa was hard. And in those times of war, life had little value. I saw a Hercules shot down by a Soviet surface-to-air missile and I learned later that it was accidental. Just as I saw countless aircraft arrive with shell holes in their fuselages, wings and flying surfaces, including aircraft with passengers.

Night flights were the most dramatic: airspace was very restricted, and landing approaches were executed with headlights and lights off. Only the essentials and at the short end would the landing lights come on and we would get very close to the operational limit. I felt unbeatable and invulnerable. Sometimes, the cargo transported was human; that's right: I transported human beings who were still alive, some without legs and others without arms. That no longer made me nauseous; I simply accepted it and went on. The smell of death became so intense that I no longer cared about its presence.

There are moments and situations in life that are not purposeful, there is no natural explanation; you are simply pushed into what has to be. I was rostered for a flight with B737-

200 Adv; and everything was ready when I was informed that, to the south of Angola, the destination airport of the flight suffered a strong attack, and the flight was cancelled. I was scheduled to go east, and for reasons not explained, the flight was also cancelled and dismissed from that day's schedule.

On arriving at the apartment building, I came across one of the maintenance jeeps, and at the wheel was Babu. He informed me that a B707 had landed and was parked in the same spot as the other one a few days ago, but it was not the same aircraft, according to my faithful African friend, but it was a B707-320F and they were waiting for me. I returned to the airport with Babu for an hour after our conversation.

There was no doubt about it, that B707 was much more preserved, with no registration number or flag, just like the other one that had landed in an emergency a few days before. I got closer and realised that it was not the same captain, but the features of the man in the left seat were those of a German. When they saw me, I think they thought I was the person they were looking for, as I was the only white person among those present on the ground.

The main door was opened, the ladder approached the aircraft and I was invited on board. The interior of the B707 was well maintained, especially near the galley and the toilet. The passenger station showed comfort for a cargo aircraft. The man I considered to be German was waiting for me near the main door, and once again I was certain of his origin. The commander's name was Kauffman and he was extremely kind and polite as he welcomed me and called me: "*Captain*". He didn't know my name, didn't ask, and nor did I have any interest in telling him. Until that moment I didn't know what they wanted from me, due to the fact that I hadn't landed in an emergency and it wasn't a scheduled technical stopover.

Commander Kauffman offered me coffee prepared by him in a normal electric kettle. My attention was drawn to the care taken with the quantity and the choice of Colombian coffee, one of the best in the world. I did not accept the coffee. The cockpit door was opened by a well-dressed, short, fat man. He left it open and came towards me, his eyes black and intense, when I distinctly heard another person speaking in a language not uncommon to my ears from the Arab world, but I could not define it exactly. The first sentence I heard from that man was: "Praise be to Allah. He brought you to me, and everything that comes from Allah is pure and good. Don't you agree?"

His argument regarding the god he worships and loves is unquestionable, but I do not believe that Allah brought me to him. My human pragmatism understood that the most appropriate response was to show education and respect; and I replied in Arabic a phrase that means a lot to a Muslim: "Peace be upon you." He looked at me deeply and asked me to sit down, while Commander Kauffman handed him a steaming hot cup of coffee.

I took the opportunity to look inside the cockpit while the door was open and was impressed with the modernisation of the interior and the conservation, for a cargo aircraft. The man's appearance resembled that of the comedian-actor Danny De Vito but with a few inches more. The watch on his left wrist was a gold Rolex, and on the other, there were flashy gold bracelets as well, plus rings on almost every finger. Commander Kauffman was a giant beside him.

After drinking some coffee and without taking his eyes off me, he asked bluntly: "Were you going to call me?"

I looked at him and realised that Commander Kauffman was

waiting for my answer as well, and I returned with another question: "And why would I do that? I don't know who you are."

That man handed the coffee cup back to the commander and asked almost pausingly: "Are you Jewish?"

I replied with a debauched smile: "No, I'm not Jewish." And once again the man appealed to Allah in thanks. I kept quiet while he spoke. His real name, I keep to this day. I call him: "*Iranian*".

While the aircraft was being filled up with fuel, he, the Iranian, told me what he did and what he needed, and finally offered me an "opportunity", as he liked to define the proposals, but not in Angola, but in Zaire, known as the Belgian Congo. I certainly did not believe all the story he took the trouble to tell, but there were some truths. He was indeed a "trader", as were his relatives, who travelled the desert on camels, and I was part of the merchandise: business does not prosper without crew members and even less so without aircraft.

Of the aircraft models he said he owned were available for cargo flight operations: a DC8-63F, a B737-200 Adv, a B707F and a Hercules. What remained to be said was where exactly the main base would be and what type of payload to be carried. These two questions the Iranian would reveal if I accepted the "opportunity" offered, but I would not leave my job for a fantasy without knowing how much the "prize" was, because at that time we were not talking about classical commercial aviation, but mercenaries.

A curious and even comical phrase I heard from him was this: "I don't hire mercenaries, but businessmen." For me it made no difference what he hired, but how much he paid to be "businessmen", without life insurance, without medical assistance, without holidays, without security for those who had a family, that is, without a future; and for this adventure to be worth every minute of my life, the payment had to exceed my expectations, but I came across something unexpected. The group of pilots was made up of convicts; that's right, men convicted of crimes that ended their lives as pilots. The Iranian was their "opportunity" to be "businessmen".

He wanted an immediate answer from me and it was the moment to see to what extent he was willing to "invest". And at first, I put some conditions, not to say demands: the two mechanics who worked with me would accompany me: he accepted; two weeks to release me from the contract: he accepted; and finally, "my price". Then he stood up and appealed to Allah.

There I realised the Iranian's weakest point: his pocket. I was sure that he was a successful man who knew how to exploit his human and material resources; besides being cultured and giving value to money as well.

He stood and, after uttering a phrase in Arabic, shook his head consenting to "my salary demand". To do better he asked me: "Don't you want an advance too?"

I coldly replied: "No."

The Iranian extended his right hand to me and shook mine cheerfully, and before we said goodbye he said: "You speak little, that is very useful, however, when you speak it is enough to be understood. May Allah protect you."

Babu was waiting for me in the car and Akin had prepared everything for the departure of the Iranian's B707. I did not fail to charge for the support services. After all, nothing was free, it was just business. I realised that the pilots who worked for him were good and demonstrated skills, not to say that they followed operational standardisation.

Commander Kauffman offered a little show of piloting

around the runway during the take-off run: he did what we pilots call "American", which consists of keeping the aircraft flying a few meters from the runway surface, at high speed, with the landing gears retracted and when crossing the opposite headland pulls the stick determinedly towards you and after a left turn with a forty-five-degree climbing inclination. That manoeuvre was outside the norm for a normal take-off. What would be normal in that world?

Kauffman was convicted of tax fraud in Federal Germany and given an eight-year prison sentence. He spent two years in prison, until his younger brother, Kruger, helped him escape one Christmas Eve. The brothers had a similar history to their Belgian and French brother in the 'life of crime' aspect, but Kruger was never arrested for his smuggling offences between the two Germanies.

Kruger told me a story when I first met him. He said that one of the prison guards had relatives in East Germany and wanted to get them out. How did he know this? His brother overheard a conversation between the guards and decided to tell Kruger, but the brother checked first to make sure that it was not a "bait" to get him. After a few days, Kauffman did not miss the opportunity to offer his "travel services" to the prison guard, and the currency would be to facilitate his escape. Kruger complied with the agreement; however, he only let his relative go to meet the prison guard after both were safely on a ship to Morocco and there they met in Rabat with their new employer: the Iranian.

The German brothers were pilots and, from Kruger's smuggling business in the criminal underworld, they learned that a businessman was taking in good pilots, preferably those who had no "opportunities".

That evening after dinner, I gathered Babu and Akin for a

business talk. Those two Africans were extremely reliable and loyal. Their work contract earned them reasonable money, not to say fair, but they were able to help their parents and relatives. Any business involving planes that came to their attention was brought to my attention for "analysis". I took care of the business planning and the profits, I kept fifty percent and they divided the difference between them; but we did not violate the basic rule of the ten per cent "rate".

Once a "client" showed up interested in a single-engine Cessna 180. Babu was always very cautious and replied that he would see what he could do. He asked Akin to find out who the interested party was. After a few days, the customer contacted Babu again to arrange a meeting where I would be present to negotiate. The customer arrived on time, and after a direct conversation, we found out that he wanted the single-engine disassembled and boxed up. We looked at each other and I decided that I would accept the service, plus the extra work that we would have to do. The customer took fifty per cent of the agreed price out of his pocket and handed it over to me. Babu counted note by note, while Akin sometimes tested one of them to see if they were not fake. It was a pleasant surprise, but even so: "When a handout is big, the saint is wary."

Distrust in a lawless world is always imperative. I promised the client that everything would be ready in seven days, and he left the premises. Babu asked me with wide eyes: "Where are we going to get a Cessna 180?"

Babu and Akin boarded a commercial flight bound for Cabinda, Angola. I was the pilot on that flight. It was no coincidence. While my faithful African friends remained in Cabinda, I was flying a B707 cargo plane to Maputo, Mozambique.

I hired a well-known businessman to provide accommodation and meals for my faithful African friends, as well as sending money to cover costs. The mission was to steal a Cessna 180 from a businessman and member of the Angolan government. That plane was a toy for the businessman's amusement. The story is this: when the MPLA took power after Angola's independence in 1975, the businessman's father appropriated a Cessna 180 from a Portuguese farmer after expelling them from their land. For that reason, I followed a simple rule: "Thief who steals from a thief has a hundred years of forgiveness." My two loyal Africans were of excellent skills. I obtained a manual for the Cessna 180, which served them as a guide, and in less than thirty-six hours they accomplished the mission.

To ship the client's parcel, I contacted a friend's cargo company in Cabinda to proceed with the paperwork. The bill for the service was negotiated and settled on behalf of other forthcoming business.

There was a high probability of an unforeseen incident, but I had always warned Babu and Akin that luck is a part of the business. I knew of the flight schedule to Cabinda, and the roster was an Angolan pilot. That pilot was the son of a high-ranking government official and openly committed one of the deadly sins: vanity.

I knew where to look for him and met him in a nightclub in Luanda. He recognised me and we went for a cold beer. Between one conversation and another, I asked him if he was interested in swapping with me, as I was scheduled to fly to Lisbon. His smile was one of total satisfaction, and he agreed. We all have weak points: his was vanity, not for the city of Lisbon, but for the lover he kept in the bohemian neighbourhood known as Chiado.

I knew the yard staff at the airports I frequented in Africa. When I was in Cabinda transporting Babu and Akin, after they left the airport I went to have a chat with one of the patio officers. The purpose was to request that the B707 be parked as close as possible to the cargo section. He immediately agreed as I put a hundred dollars between his fingers. After landing, I taxied the B707 to the agreed location and could see that Babu and Akin were in the yard, which indicated that everything was going well. Upon reaching the position, the chocks were put on the main landing gear and I released the parking brake, connected the external power supply, shut down engine number three and authorised the opening of the main and cargo doors. Suddenly two police cars burst into the airport heading for the cargo yard; I confess I felt absolutely nothing, I looked on with complete disregard, but this was no ordinary action by the authorities.

The police passed close to the aircraft and went on their way; to this day I do not know what all the commotion was about. It took seventy-eight minutes on the ground between unloading and loading the aircraft, as well as refuelling. Babu and Akin were showing fatigue, apart from their magnificent smiles. I had turned them into bullies.

The B707 took off and we were sure that this "mission" would be the first of many. Nevertheless, nothing is certain in the illicit business. The delivery of the Cessna 180 was as the client requested; and after paying the missing part, he asked: "How do I assemble the plane?" I looked at Babu and Akin and caught them laughing since to assemble the plane would be another price, without discounts of course. The client shipped his cargo and transported it east, almost to the Zambian border. My African loyalists received a significant cash reward from me. When they returned from that mission I never saw them so happy on

Angolan soil.

That evening I explained to them both about the invitation to work in Zaire and the different conditions of their current contract; however, I would get them a rewarding salary and much more. I did not fail to mention that there would be difficulties and risk to life. Babu looked at me very attentively, while Akin remained serious. At that moment Babu said something I did not expect: "I will go where Captain goes." And Akin stated next: "Captain is like Akin's brother." I had led those Africans down the wrong path, for it ran in their blood aviation mechanics; but the adrenaline of missions and financial rewards spoke much louder, yet they were grown-up enough to know what they were getting into.

I was happy about their decision and we left after two weeks. Akin went to our fridge and brought us three well-chilled beers, for he knew that among my favourites was Corona. We drank a dozen beers under the gaze of a full moon that would make any one envious, while to the south were visible the flashes of the explosions of artillery fire forty kilometres away.

Just when I thought I was going to sleep, Babu called me to tell me something that aroused a fixed idea in me. His story was this: his grandfather worked in a diamond mine for many years, as did his father; the mine was south of the town of Boma and near the Congo River in Zaire. Babu's father was one of the few who had learned to cut diamonds. The labour of that poor African was cheap to the point of being almost free, but the profit to be made by the economy of cutting and getting the best design by the hands of the African made him a specialist without renown. The African taught the art to a few under the tutelage of the Belgian imperial power, and even after "independence", the mine, the building and the cutting area with all the investments were preserved, with "participation" by the Zairean government, of course.

I didn't miss a word of his story. My mind was already planning something to the point of the impossible becoming possible when he confirmed what I expected: the Belgian company kept a deposit of first-class diamonds far from the international market and of superior quality to the mines of South Africa, whose mines were dominated by the Dutch. His father told the story on Babu's mother's birthday after drinking too much and the next day showed concern by expressing to his wife whether he had said anything about his work. She took no notice of her husband's words that night, yet Babu treasured everything.

I asked him: "Why did you tell me this?"

He simply replied: "I know Captain will have a good idea for those diamonds."

The gleam in Babu's eyes was the same as when I managed to sell a Bell UH-1 Huey helicopter parked behind the maintenance hangar. The helicopter was a forgotten relic of the Portuguese army; the "client" was brokering it for a third party. My loyal African friends dismantled the helicopter and we "exported" it through a "facilitator" at the port of Luanda by a container. The bribe was worth every penny invested. Akin's parents were able to buy some land and cattle to raise and sell in Zaire. In Babu's case, he allocated some aid to relatives and the other part he kept.

Chapter 2.

We landed smoothly in Kinshasa, Zaire, and each of us carried two military-style backpacks. A black man identified himself by name as Tousset and as the driver of a Land Rover jeep that awaited us. What caught my attention was his stature and wingspan. The African man could hardly fit into the seat of the vehicle. I sat on the right side and waited for him to address me, but it was quite a while before he uttered his first sentence. The mechanics were at "home" and relaxed. We drove two hours of asphalt road of dubious quality and another of red dirt, but the scenery made up for it.

Tousset brought water, Coke and absolutely nothing to eat, however, it was at the roadside that our driver parked in front of a commercial establishment, which was a simple house and out of it came a woman in her typical colourful dress. The skin on her face was glowing and well kept. I had no doubt that she was the owner and she then invited us in and offered us an excellent meal, which I had the pleasure of eating and paying for.

Akin and Babu got into the car and slept without being bothered by the bumps and jolts. I didn't close my eyes for anything; I remained alert and wary. Tousset sometimes pulled a conversation about football, and in a few minutes silence took over both of us. We crossed a dense area of the forest until we found the savannah wide open. About a kilometre away I saw an old military-style structure, in the shape of a hangar, next to a landing field that, by my calculation, was about two thousand metres long, as well as an area free of obstacles, which would facilitate take-offs and landings.

I took my binoculars and the first plane I saw was a Hercules. The condition of the fuselage showed little care and as we started to circle the take-off and landing area, I spotted the unmistakable tail of the DC8, undoubtedly a 63 series. Further on came the B737-200 Adv, but without its number one engine and finally, I spotted the B707, which was similar to the one I had landed in Luanda in an emergency.

The Land Rover accelerated into the last corner and swept in willingly. I woke my loyal African friends and they quickly pulled themselves together. As the car approached I saw some men appear: those were, no doubt, the Iranian's "businessmen". Away from the hangar, there was a huge fuel depot and some vehicles. I noticed certain disorganisation in the "hospice" I was about to visit. A house away from the hangar seemed to me to be the "Administration House" and it would be from there that I would give the coordinates to hell. Those "businessmen" hadn't crossed the Nine Circles of Dante's Hell, but if one of them tried to ask for the address, I would get them there by the shortest shortcut.

I immediately drew my forty-five-millimetre calibre pistol from my rucksack and positioned the comb with fifteen bullets, fitted by my gunsmith in Cape Town, South Africa, and then cocked it. Tousset's dark eyes nearly popped out of his sockets at the sight of that powerful weapon in my right hand, while my faithful African friends drew their thirty-eight-millimetre revolvers.

As Tousset was parking I saw the "businessmen" approaching: two of them with Soviet AK-47 assault rifles cocked. I jumped out of the Land Rover, and before they knew it they were both on the ground slumped over and pistol to the head of the most reluctant; the others were surrounded by my loyal African friends with ease. Tousset looked like an immobile living statue, while the sweat dripped down his face dark as ebony.

I had arrived to command social misfits, I did not expect a welcome reception, nevertheless, some men only understand the meaning of life when they meet a leader, and for these men, there is no other method of commanding but through fear. And for my objectives fear was useful to impose a vertical command; and if those "businessmen" wished to survive what was still to come, they should fear me even after they were dead.

There were fifteen men in all, including captains, co-pilots and flight engineers, plus three drunken mechanics, who were immediately removed from their quarters after my African friends got buckets of water to wake them up and make coffee for everyone. I rounded up the men that afternoon, and there was the debauched Jean-Pierre and his brother, Jean-Batiste. I knew little of their lives, however, the stories of each would be told in time. Babu brought my holster and I positioned it on my waist, under everyone's curious gaze. Akin poured hot coffee and joined his partner behind me.

The place I chose was in a room next to the hangar, as I considered it suitable and dignified. Everyone was seated and at ease, quiet and attentive. I did not make a formal presentation, this was not a company training course and the first topic I dealt with was exactly the physical aspect of each one, personal hygiene and the care of everything around them. A sentence was remembered by them for many years and in the course of living together: "It is not because you live in hell that you will turn your life into hell."

I realised that Kauffman was not present and understood that he was the "private pilot of the Iranian". And who would be the co-pilot and the flight engineer? That would remain to be discovered soon. In my personal view, there would be no privileges, no exceptions, least of all for him and his crew.

One of the first measures I took was to ask Babu to cut everyone's hair in military-style, shaved at the sides of the head, like American or British marines. Beards and moustaches were allowed, no Father Christmas as the Portuguese say. Enough to know exactly who he was.

I ordered the identification documents of each person, as well as their flight licenses, something I considered unlikely; after all, this was not a commercial airline, nor was it my intention to do so. The curious thing is that there were few murmurs. I radically broke their default routine, and none proved to be present and determined leaders; perhaps convenient influencers and far from leading men, for that rested on my shoulders.

There was much to be done before I thought of flying with those social misfits. The only certainty was in their ability to fly and on their faces was the desire to fly, however, my plans were elsewhere. The Iranian left in my hands the greatest asset he possessed. Akin went to the kitchen and returned to inform me of the general conditions. He asked permission to interrupt me with a report that did not please me. I then ordered him to do his best to ensure a decent meal for all. My faithful Akin turned around and disappeared.

Babu called one by one and shaved the sides of their heads, without complaint, and next, I ordered them to bathe and change their clothes; some were in their pants and socks. It was a calamity on the African savannah of Zaire. I warned that I would go to the lodge to check the conditions of the place.

I did not want to turn it into a prison, as it was already a madhouse, but the objective was to gain time and prepare those men for the missions that I would be planning shortly, besides which it was essential to get to know each one of them. Not every man is forged to overcome limits and I believed in the potential to be developed, which started in the imposition of fear until it reached respect and, the most expensive point: loyalty.

At dusk, Akin prepared a meal for those men such as they had not seen in a long time; besides the surprise stamped on their faces, they showed gratitude. The shortage of supplies was clear and utterly out of control. If there is one thing a man cannot go through it is deprivation of freedom and hunger. The table was occupied in an orderly fashion and I warned that everyone should share the food in proportionate portions, and I was the last to serve myself. None of them dared to ask anything, and for that day it was enough, but after the meal, I dismissed all but the five commanders. Certainly, the remarks would be the talk of the night among them.

The commanders were of different nationalities, it looked like the French Legion: Jean-Pierre, the Belgian; two Englishmen, John Brooks and Lee Greenwood; a Scot, Douglas Mcgyver; and, to my surprise, an Italian, Enrico Langoria, from Bergamo, northern Italy; at least that's what the documents showed.

Everyone's cooperation was essential for us to make money and I encouraged them for the reason they were there; after all, they were "businessmen", yet I wanted assurance that they would be paid. I heard from Jean-Pierre that their salaries were overdue. The look in their eyes and gestures confirmed the complaint and so as not to give conversation I promised I would settle the matter. That was a high-stakes gamble. If I couldn't get the wages up to date, it was better to go back where I came from; nevertheless, there are many ways to achieve a goal.

Each commander chose a co-pilot and flight engineer to form a three-man team plus a mechanic. I delegated primary tasks in order to prioritise everyone's well-being and for the first time I dared to call that inhospitable place "Base of Operations". Once the tasks were accomplished we would take care of the available aircraft, which does not mean operational. An urgent concern was the aviation paraffin tank. I was not surprised when the Scot Douglas, with his drawling accent, said that there was little fuel, yet everything was well preserved. I didn't believe him and asked for a report from Babu later. I always trusted by distrusting!

The accommodation was inhabitable condition, nevertheless, it needed repairs: the ceiling fans were inoperative, there was no air-conditioning, some mattresses had to be changed and punctures in the roof were noticeable. I considered the possibility of offering the men more privacy, especially for post-flight rest, and some entertainment, but that would take time. The strategy was to win the souls of each one so that they would be able to follow me without question when I called them since I was willing to be a leader and use them in the way I was planning.

I took the opportunity to inspect the bathroom, which in this case was collective and in totally unacceptable conditions, yet some things depend on each man, such as maintenance and hygiene. Commander Brooks recklessly remarked: "This is how we got the accommodation and bathroom."

I glared at him and asked: "And they did nothing?" The Scot could not resist his arrogant reply, which did him no good.

I prepared a list of issues to address with the Iranian: the delayed salaries, material for renovations, basic office equipment and even jungle survival. I recommended his attention to attend to everything urgently. Should denial be the answer, I would make his planes junk for sale, for which the black market was willing and available to buy. Let him not try my judgment.

Driver Tousset awaited my orders beside the jeep like a watchdog and I invited him to dinner with the other men. He was the messenger I needed. I was interested that it reached the ears of his boss everything he saw. I prepared a letter with the demands to be met, including full radio equipment on VHF and HF frequency. The list was long and necessary.

Tousset left the "Base of Operations" by the same path of arrival; my eyes followed the red dust until he disappeared. What I liked most about that place was the fenced area, like a military base demarcating a perimeter and that I considered positive; plus, a small, abandoned communications tower, according to one of the commanders.

I wanted to check the AC power generator. The noise of the generator was noticeable, indicating lack of maintenance, a matter I left to my faithful African friends, since I did not know well the other three mechanics I found drunk, however, they would be of great use assisting in the tasks ahead for Babu and Akin.

There were three vehicles: a badly beaten Mitsubishi and two Land Rover in better condition. I found a lumber yard with a sawmill that would be of great use in the most urgent repairs in the dormitory.

Each team of crew members would have activities assigned to them, and of which I would demand results. Later that night, Commander Lee in the company of Enrico came to me to inform me that the runway had some craters due to artillery mortars.

Luckily for us, low calibre shells were used. As well as there was a heavy machine that could help solve the problem with suitable fills, plus asphalt available behind the hangar. I thanked him for the information and determined to first look after everyone's welfare and then I would plan these repairs.

Finally, we all went to sleep. I went to the "Administration House" and there I found a sofa in good condition. My faithful African friends looked for a place in the house to spend the night, however, we kept watch every two hours: "Anything could happen, including nothing." The story Babu told led me to patiently fit each piece of a complex puzzle, where I would place the last piece and reach my goal. Nevertheless, this unique and valuable opportunity needed to be polished like a difficult but not impossible diamond.

The next day Akin had breakfast ready at six a.m. The men were awakened at five a.m. by the commanders of each group and led to morning gym exercises outside the dormitory. At first, there was protest from some, until I drew my pistol and fired three shots in the air and everyone took their position. Commander Enrico took the initiative to conduct a full military gymnastics session. The Italian had a military and criminal past. The men were not in shape and ended up full of aches and pains all over their bodies.

They would reach a proper physical performance in a few weeks. I had no doubts. When they arrived at the mess hall, after the gym and shower, they found a breakfast they never had; this was excellent for their morale and they all thanked Akin. I would commend the work to run as I wished and wanted.

The first group, led by Jean-Pierre, took care of the repairs and cleaning of the accommodation and bathroom, just as the mechanic got the ceiling fans fixed, cleaned and greased them.

The second group, commanded by John Brooks, made repairs to the kitchen, unclogged the stainless-steel sinks, drains and drained the cesspool. Leaking taps were made good as new; some switches and light bulbs were repaired and replaced.

The third group, led by Douglas, gathered the three vehicles in the hangar, lined them up and removed the air filters to be cleaned. They changed the engine oil of the vehicles and refuelled them properly for any occasion. Finally, they cleaned the interior in an exemplary manner with what was available, as well as calibrating the tyres with an air compressor.

The fourth group, commanded by Lee, was assigned to put the communications system back together, list what was needed for future operations and check the communications tower in detail. However, it was the fifth group, commanded by Enrico, that I was careful to deploy to group by calibre and quantity all the type of weaponry and ammunition available. As well as cleaning, lubricating and disposing of unsuitable armament and ammunition. I knew it was pleasurable for him as it was noticeable on his face. I whispered right in his ear, "Do not attempt to hide, store, take for yourself any weaponry or ammunition." He immediately wiped the smile off his face and nodded his consent.

I cannot forget to mention the names of the other crew members; the group of co-pilots consisted of Jean-Batiste, French; Igor Kracoviv, Romanian; Joseph Marcos, Bulgarian; Alex Van Klaus, Dutch; and Mark Kurt, of Irish origin. The group of flight engineers was made up of: Velasquez, Spanish; Paul Levi, Israeli; Alan Palmer, South African; Germam Holt, German; and Patrick Singer, Irish, whom I met when Jean-Pierre landed in an emergency in Luanda.

One crew was still missing, which was with the Iranian and

commanded by Kauffman. I waited for them with all my patience. They were not wasting their time. The mechanics I found drunk were Africans. I learned later that they were childhood friends. The truth: they were idle and that is fertile ground for the devil; not that a few drinks would qualify them as alcoholics, but it would keep them under my watch and iron hand.

I took some actions to continue the work, outlining a plan and checking those completed. I guided them to put the sawmill to work and they had no difficulty in doing so. The wood was used to build walls in the lodge and give the men privacy. Babu managed in a few days to overhaul the electric generator and quantify the diesel oil. The results were appearing day after day of hard work. The men were noticing the transformations. I was warned by Akin that the supplies would not be enough for more than three days and, considering the voracity of the men due to natural wear and tear, replenishment of supplies was necessary.

I was willing to travel to Kinshasa and try to communicate with the Iranian. There was the pendency of resolving the issue of salaries, as I was not interested in a revolt of criminals. But luck was on my side. After ten running days, I saw two military field trucks approaching, three tankers and, ahead of them, Tousset's jeep. Even then I was suspicious. Enrico had positioned a Browning fifty-millimetre calibre machine gun in a strategic, elevated location. He, Mark Kurt and Patrick Singer rushed into position on my command. The convoy stopped in front of the main gate which remained closed. I ordered a mechanic to open the gate.

Tousset came in his jeep and drove straight up to where I was standing. His physical size was impressive. He handed me some documents containing notes on the loading of supplies, equipment and fuel, while the trucks drove towards the fuel and supply depot under Enrico's phantom sight, since I did not want a Trojan Horse in my "Base of Operations" and much less to be Achilles: fighting so hard to die in a stupid way.

The "Administration House "continued in the same way. I prioritised the welfare of the men and then my own. Tousset accompanied me and I invited him to sit in one of the armchairs in front of my desk while I examined the documents. He handed me a package containing one hundred thousand US dollars.

Tousset looked at me and said: "It's for any emergency, the boss takes good care of everything."

And without missing the African's cue I replied: "I can imagine."

I opened a folder. I realised that the Iranian had opened bank accounts in a British bank in London. I refuse to mention the name. They were nominal accounts for each man with the deposits of the outstanding salaries. He was careful to send the respective documents proving the financial transactions. Tousset knew what this was about and asked: "Wouldn't you sell the boss's planes? Would you?"

I looked the African giant in the eye and replied, "What do you think? Let him provoke me."

I heard him whisper: "That's the devil himself."

The aviation paraffin tank was completed in an hour and thirty minutes. Next to one of the fuel trucks was a hooked tank containing enough diesel to last six months. The Iranian read my letter containing the list of demands and took it seriously, plus my promise if he refused. By meeting my demands, he quickly put me in the position I wanted: the men already feared me and would soon come to respect me. If there is one thing a "businessman" likes, it is money and any one who will take him to it as quickly as possible. Who doesn't want a high return investment in the short term? Without risks? No, there is no such thing. That is why risk is the spice of life because taking risks is not for everyone and even less for cowards.

Now I could call those "businessmen" my men. I left the "Administration House" and ordered them to help unload the supply trucks. Akin was in the kitchen directing where to put the perishable supplies, non-perishable supplies and the Corona cases of beer. My men when they saw them redoubled their spirits for the job after arduous days under an average temperature of thirty-eight degrees centigrade in the shade. The refrigerator had a good cubage, and according to Akin, it was possible to hang four stripped oxen. So were other products. The beef was enough for nine months, and it was transported in large boxes with frozen CO_2 stones to avoid deterioration by the high temperature of the African savannah.

The quantity of drinking water was sufficient for six months, but he would take other measures so that this important commodity would never be lacking. The cleaning and basic necessities would be controlled by Akin, avoiding the "black market" with the natives of three small villages around the "Base of Operations". We would establish contact with the three villages in the coming months, which would be very useful, without dispensing with caution.

All office equipment, some electrical appliances and a German VHF and HF radio of excellent manufacture, as well as antennas, were delivered. My men were impressed, and this was capital to be managed in my favour: I had a plan that included all of them, or those with the courage and eagerness to go beyond the limits of the "Base of Operations". In the early evening, the trucks set off under the sights of the neurotic Enrico.

Tousset left the "Base of Operations" in his inseparable jeep and with the trucks. Before leaving, he came up to me and asked: "Is everything as you asked?"

I once again made something clear to him and replied: "I don't ask, I order, but that's it for now."

He remained silent and swallowed dryly. It was obvious that Tousset would report every detail and the improvements in the "Base of Operations". Nevertheless, despite my harsh answer, I thanked him for his cooperation and delivered into his hands three hundred US dollars. At first, he was suspicious, but he understood that it was a simple acknowledgement when I said: "Buy a dress for your wife and toys for your two children." I saw in his eyes bewilderment and a certain joy. On the key-ring of Tousset's jeep were two photographs with the faces of two boys. I concluded that they were his sons; I think I was right. He thanked me and left.

Commander Enrico left "his hiding place" and as he approached showed satisfaction for what he called "a miracle". I made no point in refuting such a statement. I know the usefulness of a "miracle" in the lives of men; and depending on how it is performed, it can yield a lot in favour of the miracle worker, which in this case was me, according to Commander Enrico, the Italian.

I gathered the men in the same room next to the hangar and there I gave each one the documents concerning the bank accounts and the respective balances. I saw men with tears in their eyes, and others who doubted that I would be able to resolve the financial pendencies, as I had promised. They learned that lesson quickly. The dividends would be reaped day by day with interest and monetary correction; after all, as the North Americans say: "There is no free food."

I still wanted to analyse every personal document of the crew members who were with me, in addition to verifying the information given to me by the Iranian. That day Babu coordinated several tasks and I noticed that everyone was tired. So that night I decided to acknowledge their effort. Akin separated a whole piece of the beef rib as the Gauchos of the Argentine Pampas do at their best: it consists of skewering the rib vertically, sticking it in the ground and with charcoal coals at the base let it burn, what they call a gaucho barbecue. For the heat of the African savannah, nothing better than the company of cold Corona beer. Akin's first action was to put two cases of beer on ice.

Babu helped Akin with everything that was needed. My men had never experienced eating the beef like that; nothing was left but bones and empty bottles. Some men had the custom of smoking, some cigars, other cigarettes and pipes. I made sure everyone got their worldly vices; mine, on the other hand, was a good eighteen-year-old Scotch whisky on the rocks.

Babu warned me of the possibility of approaching wild animals due to the smell of meat. I considered that the perimeter was "defended" by the fence, however, I always listened to my faithful African friend. We had no incidents that night with wild animals, as the "rational animals" always find a reason for a fight.

That night of relaxation something very natural to human beings occurred: some men tried to extract personal information from me; to no avail. I do not remember for what reason, but I believe that because of the gaucho barbecue, a great friend came to my mind. His name was João Guedes, a Brazilian born in Rio de Janeiro and married to a blond, green-eyed gaucha woman, the granddaughter of German immigrants. Guedes was a B767 pilot and we met in Miami, USA, during training in the flight simulator. That friendship became a brotherhood, and a few months ago I heard that he was unemployed. His wife was trying to pay the household bills, as well as looking after a small son, whose name was Bruno.

My faithful African friend Babu had heard many stories and among many, I told that of my friend Guedes. I decided to invite him to join me in Africa and fly once again the legendary B707; however, it would be a few weeks before the invitation materialised. I had a strict military background. My friend Guedes did not. He was a big shot, the son of a big shot captain and a shareholder in a Brazilian airline. His professional "colleagues" nicknamed his father the "*Sacred Cow*", about the cows of India, since no one messed with him until the airline started to go under and layoffs occurred. It was time for a "settling of scores" with outstanding disagreements between the big boys, and the targets were the crew members' sons, and in this case, Guedes was a victim of the trail of enemies his father had cultivated during his career.

My Brazilian friend was always proud and would not let on about the difficulties he faced. The world of commercial civil aviation is very small and, one way or another, the truth comes out. Of course, I wouldn't invite him to hell if it wasn't for the money. That's all that matters for this kind of adventure: where you separate boys from men.

A few more weeks and we could start thinking about the maintenance of the stalled aircraft. The communications tower was duly repaired. I sent Commander Douglas to Kinshasa to buy a complete radio communicator; the one we had was to remain in a room in the "Administration House". Babu accompanied him as a guide and driver. In the late afternoon, they returned to the "Base of Operations" with the mission accomplished and the following day it was time to install the equipment, as well as take advantage of the existing antenna. The Mitsubishi vehicle did well on the round trip, but if any problems occurred and depending on the distance, Babu would have to find a way out.

After forty-seven running days, I called the commanders together and informed them that I would be travelling to Kinshasa the following morning. When Babu travelled with Commander Douglas I asked him to contact the Iranian by telephone and arrange a meeting in Kinshasa, since there were several issues to be dealt with, such as flight scheduling, destinations and ground support, among others. I decided that Jean-Pierre would accompany me to the meeting as an aide. The trip to the capital of Zaire went well. The meeting was arranged at the Hotel Bella Riva, situated on Avenue de La Mission and close to the Congo River.

When we arrived at the hotel lobby I asked the attendant where the restaurant was. We were ahead of schedule, so we took the opportunity to have lunch. He kindly showed us the way. The restaurant was pleasant and we chose a table near a window facing the hotel entrance. A native waiter approached and handed us a full chart for our orders, and I immediately ordered mineral water for two with ice and lemon. Commander Jean-Pierre agreed and we each chose a main course and as a matter of investment in the personal image, I suggested to the Commander to choose what he wanted and that he was not to worry about the price.

The waiter brought a varied selection of starters and I took the opportunity to ask for the wine list. As soon as it was presented, I handed it to Jean-Pierre so he could choose the wine. The Belgian guy looked very carefully and finally suggested a wine from his country, Pinot Noir type, whose name was Cavit.

The starter was tasted by us while we chatted and I learned a bit about his and his brother's life for the first time. Although I didn't ask, he told it very naturally.

The full service was brought to us and a very young helper assisted the waiter, however, the bottle of wine was opened beforehand for us to taste, and frankly, the choice was assertive. When we finished lunch we drank Sandeman Port Wine; Portuguese and exceptionally special.

At the proposed time for the meeting, we went to the reception and met Commander Kauffman, who led us to the Iranian. They had reserved a room for that meeting and with him was Kruger, Kauffman's younger brother, and the Flight Engineer Hans Marzenvic, of the same origin as the brothers. That day I met the other two members of his crew.

The Iranian got up and came to meet me. He wore expensive clothes in impeccable linen, tailor-made and of European cut. He was not a physically fit man who would appreciate the investment of the robes, not to mention the ostentation in gold and precious stones; not that it bothered me. I didn't mind. He strategically used the argument that was already becoming commonplace: "Allah, the Great Allah, has blessed us with his presence and I already know that he has turned that inhospitable place into a resort. Am I right?" My face did not move a muscle under the gaze of him, the three Germans and the five bodyguards he hired for those "inhospitable" regions.

I asked the Iranian for the security guards to remain outside the room, and with a simple gesture, they all left. From that moment on I described everything I needed to get the four aircraft flying and the time I needed. What I always liked about the Iranian is that he knew how to listen, I didn't need to take notes and remind him of what I agreed. He was always an excellent accountant of costs and benefits. He then answered me: "You will get everything you need." At that moment I realised I was dealing with someone else, a trader. If he had completed the statement with the phrase, "Don't worry," then I would have had to worry.

After a few more details and arrangements he asked me: "Why did you bring him with you?" The Iranian referred to Jean-Pierre.

I answered: "Nothing better than a witness as a herald."

And for the first time, I saw his penetrating gaze as well as his choice of words: "You would be an excellent businessman, for you know how to do something that few can do; manipulate minds. May Allah protect us from the manipulators." He gave an uneasy and unconvincing smile. Without missing that opportunity to close the meeting he asked: "Anything else?"

I replied, taking advantage of the gap: "Yes, I want the three Germans at the Base of Operations."

His answer satisfied me. However, it would not be me or Jean-Pierre who would break the news to the privileged.

When we left the hotel we ran into Tousset. He did not see us. We went to our car and drove away. I took the opportunity to buy twenty packs, each with six one-and-a-half-litre bottles of drinking water in a shop. As well as some pharmacy items: anti-inflammatories and antibiotics. On the way out of town, we filled up the car with a full tank.

On the way back, Jean-Pierre drove the car, a way to start showing confidence in him while I thought about the private conversation I'd had with the Iranian. From him, I got the plans for the flight operations that included Eastern Europe, the Middle East, Continental Africa and other regions. The cargo, for the most part, would be of the hazardous type. The B707 and DC8-

43

63 would carry out the long-range missions and the B737-200 Adv with the Hercules would distribute the cargo. He would send two tractors to the "Base of Operations", a loader to pick up and put the load on the aircraft; ideally two loaders, but I settled for one.

Everyone called me Captain. I knew there was a bet to find out my origin, this was pure teenage male entertainment. I did as if I knew nothing. Something of concern was the state of the runway. It was important to the safety of flight operations and had to be addressed in the coming days. The runway was effectively two thousand one hundred metres long. I always assumed that landing operations would occur at maximum landing weight. Pilots would need to be careful and skilful in this procedure, always taking advantage of headwinds, landing at the one-hundred-and-fifty-metres mark, considering barometric pressure, temperature and runway length. That is why we activate all the equipment available in the small control tower, even though we do not have a man trained to do so. The VHF frequency communication allowed a basic and ideal service for flight safety.

The "Base of Operations" was a military airfield abandoned by the Belgians after "independence". I did not doubt that the Zairean government ceded that inhospitable place to the Iranian "willingly" and in exchange for indirect equity participation in the "business".

The planning of the international flights was supported by the Air Traffic Control Centre in Kinshasa. When in flight, pilots would make contact to be directed to enter the outbound airway and proceed out of Zaire's territory with a bow to the destination. Most overflight clearances of foreign territories would be provided by an Iranian contractor. One serious problem presented itself among others: no telephone lines were available. "Miraculously" within a week everything was arranged by the African authority through the Iranian in the "name of welfare".

We started work on the runway. The craters were not very deep. Altogether they totalled twenty-three. The first, the second and the third group were assigned to the repair of the runway, which, although arduous, required good coordination and efficiency of service. When I delegated the runway repairs to those teams I said: "Do a good job, because this is the runway where we will take off and land."

The sun's rays punished my men; the temperature on the runway reached forty-two degrees centigrade. I ordered Babu to bring them cold beers and smoked ham and cheese sandwiches. They acknowledged my concern, however, they knew that the law applied to everyone.

After five days of the meeting in Kinshasa, I was alerted that a vehicle was moving towards the "Base of Operations". One of the mechanics opened the gate, allowing access to the courtyard. At that instant, a smile of satisfaction was drawn on my face: at the wheel was Tousset and with him the German brothers and their inseparable flight engineer and friend, Hans. All were with closed faces. I would put them in their rightful places, starting with the cancellation of the "holidays of the three" indefinitely.

The extra "manpower" was welcomed, especially with the runway repairs, which took up a good part of the day, as night was impractical due to the lack of lighting and the need for rest. The three new members arrived at a good time. I asked Babu to accommodate them in the dormitory, which already had wooden walls and privacy. The Germans noticed that the welcome was cordial and when they saw everyone engaged in their tasks they understood that "the concentration camp" was for real.

Around one p.m. my loyal African friend Akin gave the signal everyone was waiting for. My "Legion of Misfits" set off in the direction of the dining hall. They were integrated in cooperation with each other, as were the teams. However, there was still a long way to go to reach the ideal level to achieve my goal. I invited Tousset to join us for lunch. He gladly accepted.

The quantity served was the same for everyone; those who wanted more had to wait until everyone had served themselves and only with an empty plate could they ask for more. I had no problem with the food and we never had any leftovers, which indicated that enough was cooked to serve everyone. The consumption of alcoholic drinks only with my permission in order to avoid excesses. When the Germans arrived at the dining hall they had a positive reception. Almost everyone already knew each other and it was noticeable the change that occurred in the place, besides the excellent food of Akin.

Babu came up to me and said: "If I were you I would keep an eye on that one." My faithful African friend was referring to Kruger. I looked at Babu and invited him to sit for lunch, as I was always the last to be served and he understood that the remark was noted. The German Kruger was a co-pilot with a commander's profile. His elder brother was more like an "English lord", but without land and a castle, he wouldn't get past the House of Commons. After lunch my men had an hour's rest, but not inside the dormitory. The lodge, toilets and mess hall had to be clean at all times. They still had an afternoon's work; and only after the day's service was over did they clean up for dinner and rest.

After lunch, I asked Commander John Brooks to report to me on how the work was going on the runway. He joined me for a walk. Brooks put out his pipe with Dutch tobacco, as I did not enjoy smoking, although the aroma of the smoke was different. The estimated completion of services was two days. He was detailed and showed concern about the night-time lighting of the runway. Of course, it was important, however, we still had to test whether the repairs were successful: when we would assess the effects of torrential rain, wind, surface requirements for braking and grip, and water runoff. Time would tell, but I was confident.

On our way back from the walk a fight was occurring between Igor Kracoviv, the Romanian, and Velasquez, the Spaniard. I let them fight until they were exhausted and I didn't allow cheering like it was a Coliseum; I simply let them settle their differences, which came from an animosity that had been building up for days, due to their picking on each other. Sooner or later there would be an explosive moment and unfortunately, it was after lunch. Despite the energy lost, blood on their faces and dirt on them, I remembered a law of physics: "Nothing is lost, everything is transformed." Both fought loyally, this was positive: they dissipated the "negative energy" between them once and for all and, most amazingly, they became great friends. Physics helps to understand the "human being" sometimes.

I designated Commander Kauffman and the other two Germans as group six, formed by four men also, and started to work with them. That afternoon we went to the hangar where the B737-200 Adv. The aircraft was without engine number one; the wings were tilted due to the weight of engine number two. Near the side, the wall was the engine under a thick dusty tarpaulin. We carefully removed it. The engine was uncovered and appeared to be in excellent condition. I asked Flight Engineer Hans to check the numbering on the nameplate, which should be next to the Gear Box, and promptly obtained the Serial Number and Part Number. It was an original numbered engine, and this was very important since there were smuggled and black market condemned engines.

There was complete and sufficient tooling to reposition the engine in pylon number one, we just needed to plan when we would do it. I went to the cockpit with Kauffman and we checked that none of the instruments on board was missing. All the circuit brakes were pulled out, which indicated that whoever was last knew what was coming. Unused time is an aircraft's worst enemy. We had to bring a relatively new aircraft back to life.

Months later I learned the story of that aircraft: the Iranian had lent a sum of money to a cousin. As time went by the cousin did not pay the debt, which accumulated month after month. The Iranian hired Kauffman and Kruger to steal his cousin's aircraft, and they did so in spectacular fashion.

The German brothers landed the B737-200 Adv on the taxiway next to the main runway, which, as I have counted, had twenty-three craters. I wondered whether the craters were "made" before or after the four aircraft arrived at the "Base of Operations". I had my doubts about the veracity of the taxiway landing, about the B737-200 Adv and the Hercules I believed to be possible, but about the two four-engine aircraft: B707 and DC8-63. I still have my doubts, because the taxiway floor was not built to support the weight of these aircraft during landing; let's face it: "Every aviator's story has a bit of a fisherman's story."

Babu came in one of the vehicles to the hangar and informed me that the heavy machine that was helping on the runway had a leak in one of the high-pressure hydraulic hoses and that he would arrange a solution. In less than forty-five minutes I heard the unmistakable roar of the heavy machine's diesel engine, and to me, it was a sign that he had succeeded.

The B737's battery indicated zero charges and so it was not possible to start the APU. Flight Engineer Hans easily removed the battery to arrange to recharge. If such action might have remained whether the APU would complete the departure due to the downtime.

The hangar needed to be organised and they started working hard in this regard. There were moments when I questioned whether all that would be worth it, but when I thought of the story told by Babu, my perseverance resurfaced. As the evening drew to a close I realised that the next day's work promised progress.

Hans returned from a small maintenance materials room with two car battery recharging cables and a smile on his face, all dirty with dust. The hangar remained isolated from the electrical power of the main general generator. It was logical that there should be an independent electrical force. I questioned the three crew members, who immediately set out to find it. We found it and started it up, and this time, by another stroke of luck, we were successful. I say lucky because the diesel generator battery was able to start, followed by loud engine noise and black smoke coming out of the discharge with stable rotation.

The amount of diesel oil contained in the generator tank was three-quarters of the total. Next, I reached for the master switch to close contact and in doing so, it was like lighting up a sports court. The generator responded well to the electrical load requested and stood firm. Hans, without wasting any time, looked for a way to connect the generator battery to the plane battery and leave it charging, since the generator was charging its battery and now the plane's as well. Kruger and Kauffman were smiling, as was Hans. He said: "The Iranian has the instinct to know how to choose who works for him." I kept that comment as a compliment.

The discovery of the independent electrical source and the smooth running of the generator reminded me of Commander Brooks' concern regarding runway lighting. That generator could be used for that purpose; even so, we needed adequate lighting to be installed on the sides of the runway. For someone who has landed on one-thousand-and-five-hundred-metre runways with poor lighting with a B707 and DC8, lighting would come in handy, as would other priorities. I turned off the lamps that were not needed and we left the hangar while the B737's battery recharged. Later I would return to the hangar accompanied by Babu to show the "discovery" and see how the recharge was progressing. Who knows if we could risk starting the APU?

Everyone returned from the work areas for a well-deserved shower and to enjoy a good meal prepared by Akin. My African cook told me that he was preparing dinner when three natives approached the fence of the "Base of Operations". They intended to exchange goods: they were bringing fruit and wanted sugar, rice and salt. Akin knew it was a good exchange. He asked the natives to return in the morning of the next day, however, he preferred to consult me first. It was undeniable that our presence required having a stock of supplies and the natives were interested in basic commodities. I recommended to Akin a simple exchange without too many quantities on both sides, little involvement with them, avoiding unnecessary approaches and possible conflicts.

The "Administration House" lacked some care that I was slowly fixing. The room was my office, where I recorded the administrative and financial accounts in a book. No one was allowed to enter without my permission. The only telephone set that worked was on my desk with an extension with the communications tower of the "Base of Operations".

Before retiring to rest and sleep, I called Hans and Babu to go to the hangar and check if the plane's battery was recharged. In the workshop next to the hangar there were several tools and inside a drawer, we found a multimeter for testing electrical circuits. The battery was in good condition and recharged. I will never forget Hans' question: "Shall we install the battery and start the APU?" He sounded like a young man wanting action.

I replied: "And why not? But let's have a look at the dripstick in tank number one and check if there's enough fuel." There was enough fuel.

The battery was installed by Hans, while I repositioned all the circuit brakes inwards and we sat in the seats. The tail of the B737-200 Adv was pointed out of the hangar, but not uncovered. I was sitting in the left seat, I set the battery switch to ON and a few lamps came on, the charge indicator read twenty-four volts DC. I looked at Hans and asked: "Let's see if the fire extinguishing bottles are all right." I did the fire alarm test and everything indicated that it was safe and then I turned the battery switch to START and held it there for five seconds and waited. The typical APU starting noise was heard by us and the others, who ran towards the hangar; and when they got there the APU was up and running. In their eyes, there was an almost childlike joy. The window on my side was open and I could smell the burning paraffin; it was a smell that intoxicated us.

I ordered Hans to start the electric hydraulic pumps, and immediately the noise of the hydraulics working was a sound unmatched by three thousand psi pressure. They vibrated. The adrenaline of the aviator ran in the blood of those outlaws. An engine start would not be possible, that was for another day, as I still had to get the number one engine up the pylon. I ordered Hans to switch off the hydraulic pumps, then it was the APU's turn and we descended from the B737. There was only the silence of the African savannah night and from that night on, everyone knew that there was a lot of work ahead with the four aircraft and the departure of the APU heralded a new phase, which would be the most difficult.

When the runway was ready, we scanned from one headland to the other to make sure there were no foreign objects on it. On reaching the other headland we noticed the elevation concerning the other headland. This is known to us as the slope of a runway. This would be advantageous for landing when landing at the opposite headland: the elevation would help to slow down the aircraft. For take-off, it would use the higher headland, with faster acceleration over a shorter runway distance to be used. The craters were well sealed and aligned with the runway surface. It remained to be seen whether they would withstand the rain, wind and aircraft in landing and take-off operation and for how long.

The five teams arrived to help us in the hangar. At that very moment, the access road was showing the movement and approach of heavy equipment. Enrico was demonstrating war neuroses. He ran to the machine gun position and positioned himself ready to fire. I left him at "ease", but "with one eye on the priest and the other on the mass".

The heavy vehicles approached and I realised that it was the loader transport, the two tractors, two power plants, a small fuel pumping truck, to refuel the aircraft and an LPU. Without this unit we would not have started the engines of the B707 and DC8, as those aircraft do not rely on the APU. Tousset came driving his inseparable jeep and after unloading the equipment he said goodbye and left.

The tractors and loader were positioned under a deck near the hangar. The small pumping truck was parked in the sector of the fuel tank. They towed the LPU with one of the vehicles to the B707. So did each AC power plant.

The Hercules relied on APU. The assigned teams would take care of checking the operational conditions of that unit. Luck was on our side. The Iranian attended the agreement in Kinshasa; contributing to the confidence level of my men. For me it was essential.

That morning, I decided to use all the mechanics in the installation of engine number one of the B737-200 Adv. Teams one and two dealt with the B707. Teams three and four were on the DC8 and teams five and six on the Hercules. That was the only aircraft with turboprop engines. The teams' mission, under the guidance of the flight engineers, was to check the status of each designated aircraft.

The B737 is a medium-wing aircraft and easy to maintain. The installation of an engine is relatively facial. At noon Babu installed the three retaining nuts on their respective cone bolts and then securely torqued the self-locking nuts. From that moment they started connecting the fuel lines, hydraulics, electrical plugs and throttle cable from the pylon to the FCU Fuel Control Unit and to the fuel opening cable for starting the engine. Next, we released the engine climb bracket and the B737. The aircraft settled over the landing gear dampers showing lateral balance; indicating that it would not be necessary to adjust the height of the main landing gear dampers.

All was going well until one of the power plants would not start. I asked one of the mechanics to go and investigate what the fault was, while I continued to concentrate on the B737. Within twenty minutes, he returned and informed me that everything had been solved, but I did not ask what the problem was.

After installing the engine, I asked that the B737 be removed from the hangar by the tractor; however, there was no tow bar to connect the Nose Gear to the tractor. One of the mechanics opened the rear under load compartment and found inside: new tyres and brakes, as well as a towbar. I started the APU, connected the electric hydraulic pumps and authorised the push-back. The B737's tail began to move out of the hangar. It was a great victory. My men stopped to look at the B737, which was now showing life and would join the legendary old eagles and wing brothers: the B707 and the DC8.

The legendary B707 I christened him: The Black Corsair, while the unpredictable DC8 was named: The Killer Hawk. The baptism names were written on the left side and below the respective windows of the captains. Months later I learned that when the Iranian learned of the aircraft names he categorically said: "May Allah protect us! I have hired the Flying Devil."

The B737-200 Adv was as good as new, indeed. The Iranian had a jewel stolen from the air. The mechanics positioned the chocks in front and behind the main landing gear tyres after parking them next to the B707 and on the same longitudinal axis. The gauges on fuel tanks one and two showed three thousand pounds in each tank. The centre tank held five hundred pounds. It was more than enough for the testing of the engines.

I called Commander Kauffman to accompany me on the engine test as he had a good experience with B737s. Remember: stolen in the company of his brother, Kruger, as I told you. With the navigation and anti-collision lights already on and utilising conventional signals with the mechanics in the cockpit, I started engine number two and then engine number two I thought I would have a Hang Start, but the engine stabilised and remained at idle speed. All parameters were in conformity, as were the auxiliaries: AC generator and mechanical fuel pumps; nothing indicated idle problems.

I warned the mechanics that I would throttle both engines. I positioned the power levers at ninety degrees off the pedestal, with a forty-five per cent low compressor; the discharge temperature and fuel flow indicators were perfect. Next, I advised the mechanics that I would apply full take-off power. The noise from the JT8 engines was unbearable. The B737 shuddered angrily, wanting to leave the ground to get out of that "stuck bird" condition while the parking brake held it to the ground by the chocks.

I checked that everything was well adjusted and decided to reduce the power to idle. That "young man of the air" calmed down. I christened him: Angry Young Eagle. The name was written in the same position as its older brothers: the B707 and the DC8.

I ordered Commander Kauffman to test the reversers, flight surfaces, air-conditioning and pressurisation. There was no doubt, the B737 was in shape; and for the first time, we made radio contact on VHF frequency with our communications tower with full success, as well as confirming the traditional communication phrase: "five by five", which means: good bilateral communication clarity and intensity. We finally proceeded to shut down the engines and APU, as well as keeping the aircraft closed.

The next thing we knew Akin was calling us for lunch, however, it was after two p.m., and none of us minded the passage of time, demonstrating the involvement and cooperation of my men. And so, it was day after day of hard work. My concern was always flight safety, since missions at certain times would be extremely dangerous, not because of the integrity of the aircraft, but because of the hostile territories and the violence they would use to try to bring us down in flight.

The rainy season came with force, the dust turned to mud. The murderous drought abandoned the African savannah to give way to the most beautiful nature, resurfacing from every corner in a vastness as far as the eye could see. Life, which is worth little in the animal world, was reborn among young of all species, but there was no room for seasonal mercies: life and death championed the savannah hand in hand without regard for the victim. Just as they arrived, the torrential rains disappeared; the airstrip stood up to the first test. Everyone felt part of the success, and at the end of an afternoon like so many others, we were almost ambushed by a group of guerrillas who tried to invade the "Base of Operations" looking for supplies, armaments and whatever else they could find. That attempt could have meant the death of each one of us.

The leader of one of the three villages went to the "Base of Operations" as usual to trade their goods with Akin. He reported that one of his hunters had found military boot prints south of the village and that he was concerned for the safety of his clan. That day Akin came to me in the company of the village leader. I had no direct contact with him and the other members of the clan, but Akin's attitude made me think that this was something important. Akin's report worried me. Our missions were about to begin. I called Commander Enrico and entrusted him with the task of setting up a hunting and patrol group of three more men to locate the military.

Commander Enrico assigned Jean-Batiste, Alex Van Claus and Alan Palmer to compose with him the group. From his report, the information indicated that the military had moved away and the perimeter of the "Base of Operations" was secure beyond the villages. Even so, I ordered him to keep men on surveillance from a high point on the ground and with a visual field of view of the villages. With them was a vehicle with a machine gun, thirty-millimetre calibre, on the roof and well ammunition. As well as supplies and water. All my men started to carry pistols and AK-47s. I knew from the Iranian's files that Paul Levi was an instructor and strategist for Mossad, Israel's intelligence service.

That "discovery" was impactful and demonstrated, from my perspective, a conflict of interest between the Iranian and an Israeli. If there was one thing the Iranian's father and grandfather revered it was Mohammad Reza Pahlavi, the dictator and Shah of Persia. And to my utter surprise, Paul Levi was personal security for the Shah. In a bombing, from which the Shah had often escaped thanks to Paul Levi's intelligence service, he was reported: "dead". The Iranian sheltered him, to cover up the death of the Israeli, who went on with his life garrisoned by the shadow of Death. What intrigued me? Why was he given up for dead and was he hiding in? Why was the Iranian keeping Paul Levi in that hell? Time is the answer to many questions.

On a hot afternoon, Flight Engineer Germam Holt gave the alert of an invasion of the "Base of Operations" by African guerrillas. They were outnumbered and advanced in two groups with similar weaponry to ours at that time. The confrontation got off to a violent start: they used hand grenades to impress and a Soviet rocket launcher. But Commander Douglas and Co-pilot Igor Kracoviv were not intimidated and unloaded a thirty-millimetre calibre machine gun on the first group which advanced in a disorganised manner, shooting down almost half the enemy, but it was the heroic action of Flight Engineer Velasquez and Commander John Brooks which definitively contained the second group which tried to outflank us with AK-47s; they killed twelve men and cut the throats of the wounded.

The sound of the combat shots alerted Commander Enrico, who decided to abandon his position of vigilance and together with Alex Van Claus went to the confrontation zone in the "Base of Operations", but on the way, they came across two military vehicles occupied by guerrillas who were preparing to head for the entrance and join the invaders. Alex Van Claus braked the vehicle, and the upset Commander Enrico climbed into the back of the vehicle, firing the machine gun down to the last cartridge. The guerrillas fought back with the available weaponry.

I joined Commander John Brooks. He was wounded in the right forearm and the right side of the abdomen when seven guerrillas advanced towards us, trying to surround us. There was no time to think: I drew my forty-five calibre pistol, with special ammunition, the known and prohibited dum dum, and, as my father taught me at such times and despite the adrenaline: keep calm and aim to kill. The first shot went straight into the chest of one of them, throwing him backwards; the second shot hit the head of another insurgent, tearing off half his skull. The projectiles of the guerrillas' shots passed by me in an almost musical sound in that African hell.

The third shot hit his shoulder and I shot him in the head with another. I shot the fourth guerrilla through the throat, and by the effect of the type of ammunition, exploding part of his head from behind and above the nape of his neck.

The AK-47 of one of the guerrillas kept firing, but his aim did not give him the desired prize: I fired and saw the incompetent man fall to his knees. The sixth man ran away and fell, losing control of his weapon; as he tried to recover it and point it in my direction, I fired mercilessly. The projectile went through his right jaw and part of his face was torn off, while the seventh target was shooting incessantly when his AK-47 jammed, something difficult to happen with that weapon. The African guerrilla tried to engage again, while I looked at him and waited to aim the rifle again. The unfortunate man reloaded the rifle and when he tried to raise the AK-47 in my direction: I fired hitting him in the forehead and throwing him backwards with his head almost blown off. "In combat, there is no mercy for the enemy, he must be eliminated to prevent him from returning."

The adrenaline was flowing at maximum; a fierce and cruel clash was not in my plans. I looked around and there was no going back in time: land covered in the blood of men from that land. This did not please me at all, but there was no way out; it is a human conflict that lives in some and far from the mercy of a god. Commander Enrico on reaching the "Base of Operations" was overcome with despair and driven mad, for Alex Van Claus was shot inside the vehicle in the clash on the road.

The Dutchman was soaked in blood with five perforations in his body: three in the thorax, one at the junction of the shoulder with the thorax and another in the face. Enrico's cries of despair echoed through the savannah. We removed dead Alex Van Claus from the vehicle, nothing more could be done. My men took him to the hangar and on a table laid him down.

I ordered them to collect the bodies immediately and group them. That was a difficult and unusual task. Commander Enrico cursed, in his language, those souls; he dragged and kicked the corpses. I had to scold him harshly, however, the Italian drew a knife and stood in combat position. My men froze under the intense heat of the African savannah.

I learned in my military life that you never run away from combat. I removed the holster from my waistband and dropped it on the red dirt floor.

I carried no melee weapon and was willing to face him, and

what followed was his attempt to stab me. He lacked enough skill to face me, and after a few minutes, I overpowered him with a leg lock on his neck and left arm and almost dislocating his shoulder. Enrico collapsed, and only then did I let him go. I could not lose control of the situation. I immediately repositioned my holster on my waist and ordered them to leave it there and finish collecting the corpses.

The chief of one of the villages sought out Akin and asked to talk to me: honestly, it was not the best moment, however Akin appealed to the customs of caring for the body when it dies. At that moment I had a bit of lucidity when I remembered the magnificent story of the Trojan War: the value of caring for the bodies of the dead and the coins over the eyes to serve as payment to the Boatman. I asked Akin to tell the village chief that the bodies would be delivered, even though they were not from their village, and that I wanted no trouble. The bodies were delivered, I don't know where or what they did to them. I believe they were not cannibals.

That afternoon was diabolical. Babu drove a vehicle to the position where Enrico had been with three other men and brought back Jean-Batiste and Alan Palmer. Late in the afternoon, we dug a very deep grave to prevent wild animals from digging up the body of Co-pilot Alex Van Claus, the Dutchman. The body was washed on the table, we removed the clothes and the identification he kept around his neck, got clean clothes, dressed him and finally used a canvas as a shroud, sewn like a coffin and custom in the Navy.

We gathered and let them express any parting words they wished. I saw tears on the faces of some of my men; it was the feeling of humanity that still inhabited the souls of those outcasts and that would weld themselves to mine forever. The body of

Alex Van Claus was lowered into the grave for a final journey to Dante's Hell, and there he should find redemption and forgiveness, and on each of his closed eyes, I deposited a coin for the Boatman.

I uttered no word for the rest of the day. Enrico had regained consciousness and came to meet me to apologise. I had no alternative but to listen and look on with contempt despite his military skills. I kept the Italian close at all times and under absolute control. I did not consider him an enemy, however, if he attempted any action against my life I would not hesitate to kill him.

That evening I did not meet the men for dinner, I remained in the "Administration House"; but Babu brought some fruit, and I accepted it as a token of thanks. He remained sitting on one of the steps of the wooden-floored veranda like a watchdog and sometimes looked at me while I recorded the whole incident and kept the documents and identification of Alex Van Claus.

I needed one more co-pilot and casually the name of João Guedes came up. He was not a man to wield a gun, a killer, a mercenary; but he needed a good pilot. I managed to telephone Brazil and left a message with his wife that I would call her again the next day, although I did not consult the Iranian about Guedes, because I had not yet told him what had happened or about Alex Van Claus' death.

The next day I had the bloody vehicle washed, yet we continued preparations for flight operations. My men started to stay on the alert; the scene of the Dutchman's burial left them as we mercenaries say: "With the knife in their mouth."

After two days of that confrontation, the village chief sought out Akin and asked to speak to me. I accepted that he entered the "Base of Operations" and received him in front of the hangar. He was tall and always showed dignity; I greeted him with a nod of my head. That man of paused words surprised me by speaking French with good pronunciation, but the content bothered me by calling me homme mauvais, which means "bad man". The reason for that statement was that some bodies were beheaded, and to him, cruelty was not justified. I had the patience to appease what was never my intention from that armed conflict and the consequences of deaths. I handed the village chief a sum of money and he withdrew, but I asked Akin to keep him beyond the perimeter of the "Base of Operations". Money buys "human revolt".

The DC8-63F was the aircraft with the most problems due to the time it was parked, as time took a toll. I improvised as much as possible. The lower rear hold of the DC8 contained: new tyres, brakes, towbar and an excellent flight kit and essential for long-duration flights and destinations without maintenance support. The materials store was well stocked and we could consider a start date for flight operations.

I phoned Brazil and had the satisfaction of talking to my Brazilian friend. I told him what I was involved in and invited him to join my men. He accepted. I arranged the air ticket and the sending of a sum of one thousand US dollars, which I would then deduct from his income: we were friends, however: "Friends, friends, business apart."

In four days Guedes landed in Kinshasa and I ordered Tousset to bring him to the "Base of Operations". The African tried to defy me, claiming that he would ask the Iranian for permission. I simply said: "Do that, because when you leave here you will not have your testicles between your legs." He didn't dare call.

The Iranian was in London. He was woken by his aide, as

there was an urgent call from Zaire and, after mumbling words not understood by me, the unmistakable voice asked who was bothering him so early on that London Sunday morning and when he realised who it was, his voice softened, and I asked for his full attention for my account, plus the decision to hire Guedes as a co-pilot.

He listened like a good listener and agreed with my decision and said to close our conversation: "May Allah take care of their souls."

I always respected the religious choice of any human being, but I started to give answers like: "I believe that on Sunday Allah is off duty." Imagine!

He was very devoted to his god and threatened me with the fury of heaven: "Allah is merciful, but you are a blasphemer."

I finally advised that in another week we would be ready to start the missions and it was that morning that the Iranian confessed that the first flight was bound for Belgrade airport, Yugoslavia from Kinshasa on a ferry flight to Belgrade. What was the cargo to be shipped to Yugoslavia? Armaments and ammunition.

The Hercules and the B737-200 Adv would do the distribution of the cargo to the "end customers". I was advised by him that it would be necessary to use the DC8-63F, due to the availability of twenty-one pallets of cargo, however, the lower holds would remain empty.

Chapter 3.

I gathered my men and announced that flight operations would start in a week. This news caused them great emotion and I assigned the first crew: Co-pilot Kruger, Flight Engineer Germam Holt and Master Loader Babu and myself, plus Douglas as an extra crew member since it was a long-duration flight.

On returning from Belgrade the B737-200 Adv should be ready for departure and loading of cargo, so I assigned for the B737: Jean-Pierre, Jean-Batiste as Co-pilot and Akin as Loader Master. For the Hercules, I assigned: Commander Enrico, Co-pilot Mark Kurt, Flight Engineer Patrick Singer and Loader Master Mikimba, one of the Africans I found drunk when I arrived at our "purgatory". The others were to assist in ground operations with the mechanics in unloading and loading, among other tasks. And in honour of Alex Van Claus, the Hercules was named after him below the co-pilot's window.

Commander Kauffman was assigned responsibility for personnel and Commander Brooks for "Base of Operations" in my absence. Kauffman was subordinate to Brooks for strategic reasons.

The next day I had the satisfaction of receiving Guedes at the "Administration House". I did not waste any time and introduced him to the other crew members; everyone knew that he was the substitute of the late Alex Van Claus. In the afternoon I had time to talk to Guedes and between one cold beer and another, he asked me why everyone carried pistols and rifles. I told him a little about life in the African savannah. My friend remained silent and a little impressed. When I finally asked him: "Can you stand it?" I haven't forgotten his answer to this day: "If the money is good, I can stand it." Everyone has a price!

The Mabetu mechanic refuelled the DC8 to cover the non-stop route from Kinshasa to Belgrade and alternatively Sarajevo. The DC8's registration number we "stole" from an aircraft that was under maintenance in Nigeria, through the Iranian's contacts in his business world. Our flight attendant service was provided by Akin, as were the drinks in plentiful quantities.

Three days before the flight to Belgrade I called Kruger at the "Administration House" for a "business talk". I told the German that no cargo was due in the holds of the DC8 and that I was willing to bank arms smuggling in that idle space; but it was important to know the total weight, distribution per hold and cubage. I offered ten per cent of the profit upfront, as he would have no "investment" costs. Kruger had many contacts in Europe, despite being out of business, and this time he would not miss the opportunity to return to the world of smuggling. He needed a "little financial push". That was when he asked: "Can I use your phone?"

The DC8-63F was ready to start the engines when Akin contacted me on the tower radio alerting me that there was an urgent Iranian call for me. I left the cockpit and told Kruger to keep everything under control. One of the cars took me to the communications tower, where I answered the call from the extension and listened carefully to what he had to say and told him I was leaving for Belgrade.

I returned to the cockpit and ordered Babu to close the main door while the African mechanic Mikimba, another of the drunken troupe, signalled that the LPU was available. After the check-list I started engine number three, then engine number four, then in standard sequence engine two and finally number one. All systems responded perfectly. Kruger had already entered the air navigation into the FMC Flight Manager Computer and with the subsequent check-lists ready. African mechanic Mikimba showed me the landing gear and steering by-pass pins, and at 11:32 on a December day, I was aligned with the centreline of the "Base of Operations" runway that my faithful African friend Babu had painted

When Flight Engineer Germam Holt confirmed the Before Take-off Check-list Complete and Akin "cleared for take-off" over the VHF radio, I took the four power levers ninety degrees off the pedestal: the four engines roared like the "Lions of Mycenae"; and when stabilised I completed to Maximum Thrust Power as it was the first take-off of the day. The roar of the JT8-7D woke the African savannah for good, and I finally released the parking brake.

The DC8 began to race down the runway, hungry to fly. Kruger and I kept the stick forward, to prevent The Killer Hawk from leaving the ground before VR Velocity of Rotation, when I heard Kruger's voice say "V1" and then "Rotation". I pulled the stick towards me with a smooth and determined grip; the nose of the intrepid DC8 rose up like a hawk and then Kruger said: "Positive Rate of Climb", and I ordered: "Gear Up".

The hydraulics system retracted the landing gears quickly and the nose of the DC8 tried to rise by changing the aircraft's centre of gravity and I slightly compensated with the horizontal stabiliser, ceding the nose down as The Killer Hawk crossed one thousand five hundred feet quickly, due to the fact that the main cargo deck was empty. I ordered us to collect the Flaps and Slots and climb to FL150 when Kruger made contact with the Kinshasa Air Traffic Control Centre and authorised us to climb to FL390 en route.

Our approach to Belgrade airport and landing took place in the early evening with snow on the tarmac and a crosswind, nothing we were not used to despite many days without flying; but the aviator's blood is always present in attitudes and life. Commander Douglas executed the landing of the aircraft, as I would be landing at "Base of Operations", and possibly with the maximum landing weight for a runway two thousand and one hundred meters long and with several repairs all over its extension. There are no heroes, but courage is a virtue. A mercenary's motivation is money; there is no flag and no ideal.

Commander Douglas parked the DC8 in a courtyard away from the curious. The destined cargo was in a warehouse well garrisoned by heavily armed men and military cars, but with headlights off and avoiding drawing attention; only the signalman guided it into position and from there it would depart without push-back.

A power plant was engaged and we immediately switched off engine number three. A ladder was approached from the main door just as Germam Holt opened the door and leaned the ladder definitively against the fuselage of the DC8 and on it was a tall man, accompanied by an aide who carried several tightly tied parcels, which were handed to Germam Holt. My order was fulfilled: they were winter jackets, gloves and caps with wool inside, black and waterproof. Distribution was made and I advised them to note the name on the inside and they did so; the other parcels were packed near the galley.

The main cargo door was opened, a loader approached and ready to start lifting the cargo. The same tall man who came in with the packages handed Germam Holt the weight and balance calculation, however, before starting the loading I asked him to check that the calculations were in accordance with the cargo manifest presented, as well as the amount of fuel for Kinshasa. I was unhappy to see many mistakes made by aviation professionals and became suspicious of all of them.

My loyal African friend Babu checked the hydraulics, tyres and brakes. A fuel truck approached the DC8 and the driver was directed by Babu to position himself for refuelling. The truck driver connected the hoses and the ground cable to the aircraft and waited for the go-ahead to start the job.

While Germam Holt quickly checked the calculations, I took a look at the cargo manifest: the holds would not receive cargo, and the number of pallets was the exact amount the Iranian had reported. Commander Douglas was preparing coffee when Kruger called me to accompany him on a "walk to stretch his legs". It was then that the truck driver met Kruger and they talked. Everything seemed to go well.

Germam Holt came to me and said that the calculation was under the document he had been given. I ordered to add five tonnes more to the weight and balance calculations and distribute three tonnes in the front hold and two tonnes in the rear hold. He remained static and stated categorically: "Captain, with all due respect, we are going to take off over the maximum take-off weight."

I looked at Germam Holt and replied: "I know; the runway is long, the temperature is favourable, almost at sea level, and the wind is now aligned with the runway. Are we clear?"

The German was silent, showing apprehension, and then said, almost in a whisper: "Those five tonnes must be worth every ounce."

I approached him and said: "You have no doubt that they are worth every ounce, and now move your ass and have the plane loaded as quickly as possible."

Five tractors bearing the fuel company's symbol were pulling several pallets of cargo up to the DC8 when three military men would not let them pass. The driver presented the cargo documents with a hold destination, which would be a "courtesy exchange" from the transporter to the fuel company due to the price and future billing of the charge. The military asked if we knew about it. "We knew about the exchange of kindnesses." They shrugged and walked away without further question. The main deck was loaded under the guidance and care of Master Loader Babu and as soon as services were terminated the main cargo door was closed and locked.

Babu called the men from the main deck loading to load the holds with what I came to call "nostra cargo". At that moment, an "obstacle" arose. The supervisor of the loading employees wanted to know why his men were working in the holds, as that was not part of the contract; Kruger realised that it could "water down" the supervisor's interference in our business. He told me what was happening. There was no way out. I took three hundred dollars and gave orders to buy the intruder's silence: fifteen minutes passed, and Kruger had not returned; then I understood that, at the very least, the intruder was greedy.

When I got near the forward hold, the men were loading and the intruder was standing apart, near the tail of the aircraft, and a little agitated. The man was gesticulating, and Kruger remained calm. That unexpected situation could attract the attention of the military. I approached carefully from behind and looked very closely: the rear hold was loaded and the small door was open, and the cargo-raising belt still in position. I was carrying Babu's six-battery torch with me and heavy enough as a hammer; I held it firmly and landed a blow from top to bottom with all my strength before the intruder fell to the ground; Kruger held him and we quickly stuck him on the conveyor, and she did the rest of the work.

The body went up and entered for its "long touristic journey to Africa", and, certainly, to put down roots there, when Kruger pushed it away definitively and closed the door. I remarked to him: "If he didn't die, he will arrive there frozen, I will ask Germam Holt to cool the holds well."

Kruger gave me back the three hundred dollars, and I was curious to know if the intruder was incorruptible. He recounted: "The tourist on free passage wanted three thousand dollars and was charging it to the company he worked for, not him."

The refuelling truck ended its service, which indicated that we were ready to depart back to Zaire with a bow from Kinshasa. As I boarded the aircraft I found Commander Douglas asleep in the galley. I looked at Kruger and signalled for him to enter the cockpit, while Germam Holt's gaze followed us to our respective seats. Then Babu entered the cockpit after me, settled into the observer's armchair and stated: "Captain, busy night." The black-as-night eyes of my loyal African friend summed up our transgressions.

Kruger when he went to meet the driver of the supply truck, paid him fifty thousand US dollars for our cargo. He was the link to Kruger's contacts and there was no way he could lose that money to an intruder, especially to a "boss-loving worker". There was no room for cheap sentimentality. The initial capital investment would be multiplied fivefold under my management, and a portion reapplied to keep us in the running. We knew the risks and consequences, but it was worth it. Kruger was my newest business partner, not to say, partner.

At the freight yard, and under the gaze of the military and the supporting civilians, I proceeded to start the engines and from there we started taxiing to the designated headland of the Belgrade control tower. The DC8 was over its maximum take-off weight and I took every care to enjoy every metre of the runway. The magnificent DC8 remained lined up with the centreline and waiting for take-off clearance.

We were ready but apprehensive. We would only have to be ordered back to the yard to have the aircraft inspected. Then we would be in serious trouble. I remember that Babu tapped me twice on my right shoulder as if he was telling me in Morse code: "Everything will be fine."

The Belgrade control tower cleared the take-off after Kruger collated the climbing procedure. I throttled all four engines in symmetry until they stabilised, then completed full power take-off. The DC8 began to move, maintaining the axis of the runway and slowly gaining speed. My "Lions of Mycenae" were roaring furiously to get The Killer Hawk flying. The speedometer seemed "behind the times" as the DC8 raced down the runway. I could see the end of the runway coming when the speedometer pointer gained momentum and moved vigorously to V1, and once again Kruger's voice confirmed the speed we had reached, and from that moment on we had to fly to emergency procedures.

We kept the stick stuck all the way forward waiting for the VR with anxiety and adrenaline. That's what a natural aviator's blood should be when seeing the end of the runway approach. With only a few metres to go, Kruger said: "Rotation." I pulled the stick firmly towards me. The nose lifted splendidly and I maintained the climbing attitude. The Killer Hawk picked up vertical speed, allowing us to quickly retract the landing gear, and we continued to climb to FL290 en route.

The take-off was impressive. There is a secret kept by aircraft manufacturers: a manufacturer, from design, decreases the maximum take-off and landing weight by ten to fifteen per cent, ensuring operators have safety margins, yet due overhaul, inspection and routine maintenance are required. For us, it was all a matter of luck and fate. For the time being, we were destined to be lucky.

Commander Douglas awoke as we were allowed to perform a step climb from FL290 to FL310. He was carrying a mug of hot coffee. I rose from the left armchair, passed command to Douglas and said to Kruger: "In an hour and a half wake me up and you will rest." My newest business partner gave a youthful, but devilish smile at the same time. We took turns in flight, I even replaced Germam Holt for two hours in a row in the flight engineer's position, so that the German could rest, as during the landing at "Base of Operations" he was supposed to be in position. We could not predict whether we would have a breakdown at the end of the landing or even be forced into a re-landing.

Ten minutes before the start of the descent, I gave a full briefing: the approach would be from the Kinshasa blockade and with a south-easterly drift. From that moment on we were to make contact on the VHF frequency of the "Base of Operations" and wait for our "flight controller, cook and mechanic", Akin, as he would support us with basic information. It would be a visual approach and a risky landing, besides not knowing how the runway would behave when receiving the aircraft, during the roll-out to the stop. We did not have any support from the fire and rescue services in case of an accident. We were on our own.

We adopted the American procedure: when we crossed

eighteen thousand feet in descent, we adjusted our altimeters to the barometric pressure at Kinshasa airport, which should be the barometric pressure at the -,"Base of Operations" until Akin confirmed the information by barograph, as well as the runway temperature. If it was necessary to execute a pitching procedure, the power adjustment referred to this information and the elevation of the field.

As we crossed ten thousand feet, Kruger tried to contact Akin via VHF, and, to our happiness, my loyal African friend was there to help us. I decided on a long final, aligned with the axis of the runway with engines at three-quarters power ahead, landing gear lowered and locked to consume more fuel and avoid landing beyond maximum weight. By my calculations, we were inside a safe and convenient ramp. The checklist for landing was complete while Kruger awaited my Full Flap Down command.

The DC8 was consuming fuel at low altitude, engine ahead, plus the parasitic resistance purposely caused by the flap and landing gear, and when we were approximately a quarter nautical mile from the headland and five hundred feet altitude, I ordered Full Flap Down and I increased the power to maintain the speed to cross the headland.

On crossing it I progressively and determinedly withdrew power from all four engines in symmetry and within fifty feet of the ground, the DC8 was in the correct flight attitude and ready to touch down on the runway. Passing twenty feet I pulled slightly on the control stick maintaining the flight attitude until it touched the runway and received the main landing gear. I activated the spoiler control, then gave way to the nose and the Nose Gear tyres touched the ground. I applied the brakes and quickly reversed all four as my "Lions of Mycenae" roared to warn of their arrival on the African savannah. The DC8 stopped a hundred metres from the end of the opposite landing headland and I entered the taxiway.

During the taxi, I noticed that the B737-200 Adv and Hercules were positioned properly for immediate departure after being loaded with cargo from Belgrade. The "Base of Operations" was now our cargo distribution airfield. The Hercules was fuelling, and my men were carrying out their duties to ensure immediate departure as ordered, as well as showing cooperation.

The B737-200 Adv was next to the Hercules and from the time of day I figured it had already refuelled. As we approached the large yard, I executed the back-track manoeuvre, passing the right wing in front of both aircraft and under the eyes of all. Finally, after the ground procedures, we switched off the engines and I authorised the opening of the main cargo and passenger door. I asked Babu to come to the cockpit, as I had a very important matter to discuss with him. Naturally, Kruger knew what this was about.

All cargo was removed from the DC8, except for that in the holds, while attention to the other two aircraft consumed the work of my men. My faithful African friends, Babu and Akin, removed the body of the "tourist", carried it to the DC8's landing pad and buried it, after digging a deep grave with the heavy machine to avoid wild animals.

The nostra cargo was removed and positioned in the hangar and covered with a thick tarpaulin. The Hercules cargo received pallets with boxes of AK-47 rifles, ammunition, anti-tank missile launchers and RPG-5 projectiles, boxes of mortar launchers and their respective mortars. That was the "menu" that the Iranian was offering to anyone who wanted to buy. I was getting into the arms-trafficking business without interfering in other people's interests, but I would use the structure; after all, I was not "stealing" from him, just "borrowing the planes".

As I said, I assigned to the B737-200 Adv: Jean-Pierre, Jean-Batiste, the co-pilot and Akin, the master loader and African mechanic. The cargo's destination country was Namibia, south of Zaire, for which the B737 would invade and cross Angola's airspace and make an assault landing on a one-thousand-two-hundred-metre dirt airstrip. It would then perform a back-track at the opposite headland, stand there to unload and be ready for take-off.

The B737-200 Adv is equipped with an APU with a pneumatic and AC power supply, yet I ordered Commander Jean-Pierre to keep engine number two running during unloading from the main compartment, and only cross-bleed engine number one and use the APU if there was no alternative. The reason for that decision was precaution, for if an APU failure occurred with the engines shut down, they would remain isolated in the middle of nowhere. That was if they were not killed, and the plane dismantled and sold in parts to the first African smuggler who came along. The landing operation would be a big test for Jean-Pierre.

I assigned Commander Enrico, Co-pilot Mark Kurt, Flight Engineer Patrick Singer and Master Loader and mechanic Mikimba as Hercules crew members. The cargo's destination country was Uganda, however, just like the B737-200 Adv, they would also make an assault landing on seven hundred metres long dirt road with no possibility of back-tracking. The instructions were to land and stop before a small bend in the road. The other stretch of road was for take-off, unfortunately with a hundred-and-eighty-metre-high hill at the axis of the road.

The fuel was in the exact quantity needed to fly to the

destination, unload and take off again without refuelling. We were certainly not an exemplary commercial airline.

There was no doubt that my crew was tired, but we would only rest after the other two aircraft took off. Both landing operations had to take place during daylight hours and without beaconing or any means of landing guidance. The skill, daring and courage associated with the bank account made each man invulnerable and marginal to the rules of flight; but as I said: "We were not an exemplary commercial airline." The B737-200 Adv was lined up with the centreline, when we heard the two JT8-D engines accelerate to full power, run down the runway and energetically lift the nose up quickly and into the low cloud to the left.

The Hercules positioned itself aligned with the axis of the runway and waited a few minutes in order to avoid the wake of turbulence generated by the engines of the B737 taking off ahead. Enrico accelerated the four engines of the old turbo propeller and began to move down the runway gaining speed. After a few seconds, he lifted the nose and climbed up. I don't forget Babu's comment: "They were both heavy, very heavy." I looked at my faithful African friend and said to him: "This is just the beginning. We will work hard, but we will make a lot of money."

My men were now doing what they loved in their lives: flying! I made sure that the payments were always on time. But I needed to make these men "real businessmen", in other words, to make them "my mercenaries". And for that, it was necessary to move on to the next phase: respect. Everything I planned and determined was carried out to the letter, and my men's involvement in all tasks, under my command, assured them of being led. Although they feared me, respect aligned them to my goals. I needed them, yes, but as well-paid, brave mercenaries, loyal to me and my command.

I realised there was much to polish in order for my plan to succeed and everyone to get the share I would determine for each; however, they had no idea what I had in mind.

Planning an operation or mission gave me great pleasure. Success depended on many variables, and two of them I had control over: my men and the aircraft. They realised that the holidays were over from the moment I arrived at the "Base of Operations".

The B737-200 Adv crossed into Angola's airspace without overflight authorisation, let alone a flight plan. I have already said that we were far from being a model commercial airline and I even believed that the B737-200 Adv would be intercepted by Soviet fighters in Angola, but the Angolan air defence was not worried about a B737-200 Adv because the TAAG fleet, Angola's commercial airline, had several planes of that model, and the airspace control centre was inefficient. I was counting on these "weapons" and "possibilities". The rest was luck.

The B737-200 Adv began its descent after stalling vertically at Rundu, Namibia, and veering off on a south-westerly heading of approximately ten nautical miles. The plan was to attempt contact via VHF with a prearranged radio frequency. Jean-Pierre followed the entire plan until he switched to visual flight with the Okavango River behind him. They could not see the landing site, although they knew that a small farm was on the right-hand side of the designated road. To Jean-Pierre's relief, a jeep emerged from a side access indicating the "landing strip".

To the dismay of the crew, the runway length was no more than eight hundred and fifty metres. Jean-Pierre crossed at a thousand feet over the small house and began to pull away to execute a thirty-degree turn to the right. When he visualised the "headland" of the road where he intended to land. The B737 continued to descend with the landing gear lowered, braked and Flap 15°, the power levers three-quarters ahead, crossing seven hundred feet to enter the short final at maximum pitch. He pushed the stick forward to continue descending, undid the lateral pitch quickly and aligned with the road axis with Flap 25°. He throttled the engines, and, realising he was guaranteed a landing, ordered: Full Flap Down; and a few feet up made the B737 touch down on the dirt road with the main landing gear and after with the nose gear of the plane. They immediately applied the brakes and reversed the engines causing a "cloud" of red dirt to come to a complete stop.

What was left of the road was seventy metres, but with room to perform the back-track and line up for take-off. Commander Jean-Pierre proceeded as ordered and kept the B737 ready, but before opening the main cargo door, he ordered them to keep their weapons engaged and ready to spring into action if necessary.

The jeep approached the B737 under the gaze of the crew members and after one of the men signalled in the direction of the house: over thirty armed men ran towards the aircraft; those were the "unloaders" from the main cargo deck. Akin reported that within thirty-eight minutes the main cargo bay was empty, something impressive given the amount, weight and volume that was removed, and without a single piece of equipment to assist them. When the last crate of weapons and ammunition left the B737, the jeep and the men disappeared into the bush.

Jean-Pierre wasted no time starting engine number one, then accelerating to maximum take-off power due to the unconventional and extremely short runway. They still had the challenge of crossing into Angolan airspace, and we had to provide lighting to land on the "Base of Operations" runway, as it did not yet have its own lighting.

The B737-200 Adv was scheduled to arrive at night, and as soon as they left the "Base of Operations", we arranged to open holes at the sides of the runway, approximately twenty-five meters apart; we added wood and fuel. When Jean-Batiste made contact via VHF with our radio we set fire to the material in the holes along the runway and including the beginning and end of each headland. The approach of the B737-200 Adv went well, with the aircraft landing headlights during the final approach, landing and taxiing to the yard. The first mission of the B737-200 Adv was a success, despite some difficulties.

When I met Jean-Pierre and the other crew and mechanics already on the ground, I greeted each one and to relax I asked the Commander: "Have you delivered the goods? Did you get the delivery receipt?"

The Belgian turned pale and replied: "Sorry, was that to get the delivery receipt?" The laughter was loud and general. He didn't know how to pull himself together from such naivety.

Some men carry their luck with them, others drag the chains of bad luck. The operation in Namibia would take longer than the one in Uganda, however, the Hercules had not returned, and up to that point Akin had received no radio contact by VHF or HF. I did the calculations, and from the time it indicated that something didn't go the way it should. However, there was a phrase I always used: "Anything can happen, including nothing."

The Hercules kept the west bow and when I sighted the Lake Albert it should cross it and land between Butiaba and Masindi, in the only available road. The guidance for the location was through a radio navigation aid near Butiaba. Commander Enrico had the support of his co-pilot and flight engineer. After crossing

Lake Albert, they followed the orders and after five minutes away from the lake, they spotted the road. The departure procedure was standard, and the commander began to do so by visual navigation, and the weather helped as there was no significant weather condition.

A left turn allowed Commander Enrico to see the flight and landing area. The Hercules with Flap already extended and with the power levers at half-stroke and in a curve continued descending. The aircraft was crossing a thousand feet when he ordered landing gear down. At that moment the nose gave way down and, without wasting any time, he accelerated all four engines in symmetry. The Hercules was flying in the opposite direction to the landing. Commander Enrico knew that the "runway" allowed no chance for error; indeed, to err would be fatal.

The Hercules executed a short breakaway and initiated the turn to the base leg, to engage in a final, tight short, passing over some trees, and diving to land in the first few metres of the "runway". Commander Enrico lined up with the non-existent axis of the road and ordered: full flap down. And finally, he landed making the mighty Hercules brake with everything, including the propeller flap and hydraulic brakes of the main wheels, when a missile crossed the front of the cockpit and by millimetres did not explode the aircraft.

What followed was armed combat between the groups facing each other in Uganda. The insurgent group wished to receive the ordered armaments. The crew abandoned the aircraft to take refuge in the low ground, despite being armed, when a Soviet T-52 tank burst through the thicket, covered in heavy foliage and aimed its powerful cannon at the Hercules. An anti-tank missile shot out from among the trees on the left side of the road and hit the turret, setting it on fire and exploding the diesel tank. The fight went on for over forty-five minutes, between mortar and machine-gun fire imposing on the advance of one of the groups. The Hercules received more than thirty shots during the landing approach, and on the ground the precariousness was notorious.

The group of military personnel that approached the Hercules was the one that would receive the weapons load. I learned later that they were several combat and opposition groups; something very complicated, as they were all similar in appearance and armaments used. Weapons do not choose the hands that are going to use them. The weapons we were carrying were suitable for any combat group, but we could only deliver them to those who paid the Iranian in advance.

A "weapons lord" has no ideology, no flag, and even fewer feelings. The situation of the Hercules crew was difficult. Whose wouldn't it be? But it would be up to the commander to make the decisions, and for the African combat group, the goal was to take possession of what was theirs.

The unloading of the Hercules was very efficient. Just as the Africans appeared to claim the war belongings, they disappeared, not caring about the lives of the crew, as they considered them vultures of the African savannah. Commander Enrico had no alternative but to try to take off facing a hill one hundred and eighty meters high, on a road four hundred meters long. It was suicide. Co-pilot Mark Kurt was experienced in piloting the Hercules and asked Commander Enrico to let him execute the take-off.

The commander's position is dramatic in the cockpit. There are times when listening to a fellow pilot requires humility. In the situation, they were in there was no room for pride. Commander

Enrico authorised the take-off by Mark Kurt's hands after looking at Flight Engineer Patrick Singer and he agreed with the positive sign with his right thumb, but at that moment Flight Engineer Patrick Singer noticed the missing Mikimba mechanic and alerted Commander Enrico.

The crew members left the cockpit and went in search of the African mechanic but could not find him inside the aircraft. A trail of blood was followed by the three and what my men saw was something horrible but real. Mikimba was hit by a shot in the stomach during the approach to land, and on leaving the aircraft, his blood still warm, he ran in desperation through the bush towards the combat group who, on seeing him wounded, did not recognise him as one of their fighters: they murdered him by piercing his abdomen with a long knife, disembowelling him still alive and finally cutting off his head.

That Dantesque scene destabilised Commander Enrico, and the beast that lived in him awoke a thirst for revenge and to kill, but it was Patrick Singer who stopped him with a tremendous punch that made him faint for hours. There was no alternative. Mikimba's body was taken inside the Hercules. My men decided not to leave him as remains to be devoured by wild animals. That act was one of courage and respect. Co-pilot Mark Kurt carried Commander Enrico on his back to the Hercules, settled him on the floor of the main cargo bay and prepared for the take-off of the aircraft now christened: Alex Van Claus. The four-man team was now restricted to fifty per cent and with the mission of taking off in precarious conditions on a short "runway" and facing a hill one hundred and eighty metres high.

Mark Kurt had no choice. With all four engines at full power, he released the brakes and the Hercules began to race down the road. Less than forty metres from the finish he determinedly pulled the control stick into a near stall attitude and kept it on the limit, struggling to gain altitude, while Patrick Singer assisted him by immediately retracting the landing gear, thus allowing the Hercules to gain altitude and pass within a few metres of the top of some trees.

I confess, that I almost considered Hercules' first mission a failure. My men had never seen me so quiet. They perceived in me a man with some humanity. The truth of the facts was a card I used with great versatility because it was the opportunity to "add up points" in my favour and use them for my objectives: to weave a web carefully, which meant, in the future, a single chip play, but with the certainty of winning.

Four hours after the landing of the B737-200 Adv, my faithful African friend Akin came running to warn me that Patrick Singer had made contact via VHF radio: they were twenty-five nautical miles from the "Base of Operations". My men were waiting for orders: "What are you waiting for? Light the fires immediately." But when Akin informed me that the Hercules was in an emergency: with hydraulic breakdown, number one engine inoperative due to oil leakage and number two engine inoperative due to propeller firing due to gearbox damage, I realised the gravity.

The Hercules was struggling in flight with three malfunctionings. The worst would be controlling the aircraft on landing with two engines, and should it need to pitch it would not be easy. Akin completed the picture when he informed me that the landing would be performed by Mark Kurt in a night flight without approach and landing aids.

I saw the navigation and anti-collision lights of the Hercules appear on the horizon. Mark Kurt initiated a turn with a wide departure avoiding inclines of more than fifteen degrees. He positioned himself on a long final, however, it would be necessary before the Hercules crossed the headland for Patrick Singer to command to zero the Rudder's position as by decelerating the engines the aircraft would tend to drift off the runway axis. The landing lights were lit on passing five hundred feet altitude; the runway was well lit, while the men waited at the opposite headland expecting the worst.

The Hercules crossed the headland, raised its nose slightly and touched down on the runway. Mark Kurt proved to be an ace, and there he earned all my respect. The Hercules went to the intersection heading straight for the yard, executed the back-track, cut the engines and waited for a power plant. The brave Hercules had projectile punctures of various calibres everywhere; the damage to the structure of the battered plane was noticeable, demonstrating the warlike violence. The cargo door was opened and the electric power plant was immediately connected to the aircraft, as for some reason the APU was inoperative.

There are moments in life that remain in our minds forever. My instincts guided me not to let anyone into the aircraft. I spotted two bodies on the cargo floor, one of them was Commander Enrico, who I thought was dead and face down. When I made my way inside the Hercules, I realised he was alive and with his hands tied back. Flight Engineer Patrick Singer walked towards me with a lost look on his face, but with adrenaline in high doses in his blood. He pointed to the tarp covering a body. I crouched down and removed part of the tarpaulin and saw the decapitated body of the African mechanic Mikimba. There are no words to describe the cruel reality.

Co-pilot Mark Kurt left the cockpit and said: "I couldn't leave him behind." The other men dared not enter the Hercules without my permission. As Enrico tried to free himself from the restraints on his wrists, Patrick Singer lifted him off the floor and held him upright.

I approached Enrico closely and calmly asked: "What have you done? You owe me a very detailed explanation."

Mikimba's body was buried at dawn with everyone present. We could not leave the body exposed for long due to the heat of the savannah and the smell of flesh and blood. It was a quick and respectful ceremony. The cargo compartment was washed by some of my men, in addition to structural and mechanical repairs, which included the number one and number two engine urgently. On the same day, I ordered Patrick Singer to prepare a report of the material and all that was needed for the urgent repairs to the Hercules, in addition to communicating to the Iranian the death of Mikimba and the state of the aircraft. Despite everything, the two missions were a success in terms of accomplishment.

I had to reassess my plans for the delivery of our cargo, as the buyers were already eager to receive it, and we for the payment of five times the total amount invested, including bribes. The profit would be two hundred thousand dollars net discounting the fifty thousand dollars when we delivered our cargo. Of course, the Iranian would not see a penny of my transaction, but in the business world there is always a "big mouth" and there is always a way to close it too.

The Hercules was towed into the hangar and they did everything possible to advance the maintenance services, but we had to wait for the replacement material. At the end of the afternoon, I called Mark Kurt at the "Administration House" and asked him to tell me what had happened, as well as requesting the presence of two other pilots as witnesses. It was not a court of law, but the control of my men depended on my determinations.

The account was blunt and straightforward. When he finished, I thanked him and, without dismissing him, called Commander Enrico, from whom I asked for an account of what had happened. I cannot deny that the highest authority in a cockpit is the flight commander. His piloting skills were described as very good by Mark Kurt, even though he was emotionally out of control in a conflict and crisis, which in this case did not concern the cockpit. The vision of a commander cannot be monocular but must be all-embracing, what I call "three hundred and sixty-degree vision".

Finally, I asked Flight Engineer Patrick Singer to report on what had happened. Patrick's speech was twice choked up by Mikimba's death. They had not been friends for years, but the African mechanic was well-liked and competent and had professional respect and admiration for the African. When he referred to Commander Enrico he did not spare the words of contempt, something natural to his outlook for the type of mission we were involved in, and summed up with this question: "What guarantees can Commander Enrico give? This is the second time he's lost control." It was the questioning I needed, but from the mouth of another crew member, and from that moment on I would make a definitive decision regarding Commander Enrico. In order not to appear hasty I considered twenty-four hours to manifest myself.

The comments among my men were natural, for them, everything was a bet. Moreover, they desired from me a demolishing attitude; they nurtured something that in definitive would demonstrate if I really was the "bad man". I always had in mind that there are two ways to educate a human being: "by love or by pain". I had not the slightest interest in educating men looking for fortune, however, it was the opportunity that I had received "hands down", and I could not waste it. Commander Enrico was a neurotic and ambitious man, to the point of removing any obstacle in front of him. I was an obstacle.

There was a golden rule among mercenaries: no violation is admissible within the group, that is, theft and robbery, mainly. Even though Enrico did not violate any of them, he was a potential threat and in that case, there are alternatives: the first; "keep your enemy under your gaze at all times", the second; "if you are going to eliminate the enemy, do so never to return", the third; "live with the vipers". I'm not fit to be a candidate to guard the gates of the madhouse and I do not like to live with those who can be lethal to me. I stayed with the second alternative.

The first step was to eliminate Enrico's financial rear-guard, and with that make him fragile; to make him break one of the golden rules was my objective, and with that defeat him. I don't care if it is a deplorable attitude, I am not willing to put at risk my plans, which included all my men and the division of profits. We were not on a "docile tourist safari".

I gathered my men together in Enrico's presence and communicated that he would no longer participate in the missions and that in a few days he would leave the "Base of Operations". He would not receive the extra payments and was restricted to staying between the barracks and the mess hall. What I expected happened: the Italian stood up explosively, and, between threatening words, he dared to draw his knife once again. My men did not have the patience that was characteristic of me in moments of crisis, chance that my war name was Iceman. They stopped him immediately, and that night Enrico slept tied up. My certainty was that he would commit a golden rule violation.

Enrico was released in the morning. That day was intense as we were preparing the B707 for a long-distance flight to Baku, USSR. I considered that flight dangerous and extremely secretive; to the point that the destination of the cargo in Baku was not known to the crew. Before long, Babu came to me and told me that one of the crew members had stolen some money. I had no doubts: "The fish dies through its mouth."

The Co-pilot Joseph Marcos had kept with him the sum of five thousand dollars, it was no secret to any one, and the best place to keep money is among your peers. Banks rob you legally! And it wasn't hard to find the thief. Enrico had anticipated when he prepared to leave the "Base of Operations": the Italian had a double-bottomed suitcase and nobody knew it. I decided on an interrogation accompanied by some of my men; and his first reaction was to deny it, in the same way as when you catch two lovers. What he never imagined was that we would bring the suitcases and go through them, but it was Flight Engineer Paul Levi who, through his experience in Mossad, detected with great skill the double bottom of one of them, and there were the five thousand dollars.

My choice of the "second alternative" was assured and it now remained how to eliminate him. On my face, there was not the expression of satisfaction, but victory over an adversary for human weakness. My men knew that one of the golden rules was broken by Enrico and there would be no leniency. The news ran like gunpowder fuse, and in a few minutes they were all gathered in front of the "Administration House" I ordered him to be bound by his feet and hoisted until his head remained at the height of my knees.

I removed my holster and shirt; then I closed my fists and delivered powerful punches to the kidneys. At first, he resisted like a rabid dog, but as I struck him hard, Enrico gave in and blood began to flow from his mouth and that's when I didn't slow down, for my aim was to eliminate him and consecrate myself definitively as the "bad man".

He died that afternoon. We buried him without mercenary honours, and the money was returned to the owner. Was that justice? No, it was not and never will be. Fair? Yes, under the circumstances. Enrico would never come back to try and eliminate me, not today, not tomorrow and not ever.

My men did not utter a single word about what they witnessed, and I never demanded silence because I never had to. They knew that I knew the life of debtor and outcast that each one had. There is something that eases my conscience to this day, Enrico was a cruel murderer: on his "curriculum vitae" was the murder of fifty-three people in a village in Mali, including fourteen children. One doesn't pay death debts with more death, however, for Enrico, and all of us: "The planting is optional, but the harvest is obligatory."

I placed two coins over his eyes before he was buried so that he would not wander through Hell without seeing his destiny. So, the Boatman carried his soul across the River Aqueronte, where Cerberus was waiting for him at the gates of Hades to be received by the Devil in Hell.

Chapter 4.

I promoted Mark Kurt to commander. Life in the African savannah was not quite what João Guedes expected and he was impressed with my lethal attitude. In the evening he sought me out at the "Administration House", and I confess that I have never forgotten the expression of repudiation of what he witnessed. I listened to the last word, with patience, and said with total calm: "You haven't seen anything yet, but the door of the street is the door of the house." He left the "Administration House" enraged, but I knew him very well; I hadn't invited him to spend his holidays at a resort and he was the unemployed one.

João Guedes was a good pilot, but no better than me. We were friends and he was the only one who dared to challenge me and say what he thought, but I annoyed him with a debauched and juvenile smile on my lips. And it was precisely him who once gave me the name of war: Iceman; the reason he claimed was my coolness in flying. João Guedes openly commented that I was a "bird disguised as a human being". What impressed him most were the precise manoeuvres and assertive decisions in flight, to the point where he was a little envious. In time he realised that he would never outperform me.

I climbed into B707: The Black Corsair: Commander John Brooks, Co-pilot João Guedes, Flight Engineer Paul Levi, Master Loader and mechanic Babu and myself; the destination was Baku, USSR. That was the B707's first flight on a mission and overflying politically complicated countries. And which wasn't? We took off on a ferry flight from the "Base of Operations" when it was still dawn on the African savannah. The procedures were similar to the mission in Belgrade.

The take-off run of the B707 was fabulous, with a take-off Flap 14°. The four-engine jet performed in exemplary fashion climbing to FL390 via the Kinshasa Air Traffic Control Centre. Departure from the African continent occurred after flying over Port Sudan, Sudan, and bowing out of Baghdad, Iraq. I can't forget Paul Levi's comment: "We could fly over Tel Aviv and I'd miss you."

I asked: "Do you think your brothers don't know that we are flying with a Baghdad bow?"

I never sympathised with Israelis and I had plenty of reasons; don't confuse anti-Semitism with anti-Zionism. Paul Levi was different, but I didn't trust him; there was something that unsettled me, yet to be revealed. When I met him I knew about him from the Iranian's reports. He always showed co-operation and interest in all the tasks to which I had assigned him. He was, in my view, a necessary and useful evil. I don't trust Israelis, especially not a former Mossad.

Two hours after the B707 took off it was the turn of the DC8 bound for Prague, Czechoslovakia. The flight Commander was Kauffman, Co-pilot Kruger, Flight Engineer Velasquez, Loader Master Akin and the African mechanic Tatus. Days before that flight, I talked to Kruger about business and tasked him with continuing to conduct the smuggling transactions, but this time from Prague.

The flights were not regular like on a commercial airline; I realised that was one of the Iranian's strategies. This created difficulties, but I received in advance what the "flight schedule" would be and with this advantage, I had a much more valuable card than an ace up the sleeve, which gave me time for planning with Kruger.

The same day I took off for Baku, USSR, the B737-200 Adv made its first flight with our cargo, bound for Mogadishu, Somalia. This flight was commanded by Jean-Pierre and the Co-pilot Jean-Batiste as crew members only.

Those operations were very risky. It was enough to ground the aircraft, take the cargo and kill the pilots, but anyone who dared knew there would be consequences for being mercenaries: "If you like golden eggs, take care of the hen that lays them." Our cargo consisted of shipments of weapons from several countries, including the Western world, as well as plenty of ammunition. As I have already told you: the final price was five to six times the amount paid to the middleman. The cost of fuel was on the Iranian's account since he learned that the paraffin he sent to the "Base of Operations" came from production deviations under the banner of bribery. If for him the price was what he paid for the bribe, nothing fairer than to provide me with one of the "slices of the cake".

The Iranian did not know about my "company" and had no percentage interest in it. The cost of the operation was zero; apart from the indirect financing using the hundred thousand dollars I received for emergencies. Excuse me, I could not leave the money with no income. The mission in Mogadishu went well by African standards, however, Jean-Pierre only opened the main cargo door after counting the money with his brother. They received two hundred and fifty thousand dollars; of these, fifty thousand dollars went back into the accounts he kept, and in cash: a net profit of two hundred thousand dollars.

From that moment on we needed to give our investments a

safe destination and of course, it would not be through an ordinary bank; it was not much money to debut on the off-shore scene, however, there were tax havens available to kindly welcome the investments.

The flight of the DC8 to Prague was part of a well-planned series of smuggling essentials into the world of war. The biggest producers and sellers of arms are the very countries that have captive seats on the UN Security Council.

Problems would certainly arise at some point, and nothing would remain secret as in a tomb; that is why we had to act quickly and competently. The "profits" would be divided fairly, but I do not deny that I always had a significantly higher percentage, besides the fact that my decisions were not to be voted on, but respected; after all, this was not a democracy.

The flight to Prague had other objectives for the Iranian, as in addition to the contracted military cargo, material for repairing the Hercules was also on board, as well as two Czech mechanics for structural repairs. I needed the Hercules for the distribution of the Iranian's cargo, including our cargo. The cargo holds of the DC8 were crammed with our investments. Kruger took care of paying our "cargo agent" in cash, and he knew better than to ask for an invoice.

The investments thickened the business's equity and soon we would not be dependent on third parties. What about our own fleet? I confess it was something I thought about, but it was not my priority yet, possibly further down the line. I followed a maxim: "Who wants everything ends up having nothing." I think it is only when one reads Zurich's Axioms that this maxim is understood, but sometimes there were temptations, just like chocolate: "If you don't know how to taste it, you lose the pleasure."

My faithful African friend Babu has always loved helicopters, and once again he brought me a subject that I analysed very carefully. The African told me that there was a place in Gabon where military personnel sold helicopters that were to be "discarded", which indicated that a new shipment would arrive to replace the "discarded" ones. What Babu proposed was to steal one of those new ones. I listened carefully to every word, however, for that mission, we would need the Hercules and technically all the men to provide cover while we loaded the aircraft. The structural repairs would take a few days, the time I gave Babu to present me with a logistical plan for the mission. I offered no guarantees of carrying it out. The African knew that if he decided to go ahead, it was a sign that he had already studied every detail.

In the world of arms smuggling, it always involved cash transactions. My grandfather always said: "Where there's money there's always trouble." Wrong. I don't buy problems, I buy solutions, and money was part of the solutions; and when my men started to see the money coming in, they realised that they were in an active business "company", which became their motivation; and it could only be because they were mercenaries. Time is something extraordinary, for it was through it that I got to know each of the mercenaries I commanded.

As we penetrated Soviet airspace, we were escorted by two Mig-25 fighters. That fighter was one of the most feared war machines of that time. The escorts parallel to our cockpit were maintained up to fifteen hundred feet altitude during the long finale, but each opened a sharp turn in the opposite direction to reposition themselves in escort, however, farther back behind the B707, and as we crossed the head of the runway, the two Mig-25s accelerated, gained altitude to scramble through the clouds and disappeared.

As we left the runway and entered the first intersection we reached the taxiway, where a military jeep was waiting for us. One of the occupants told us to do a back-track so we would be ready to go after loading and refuelling. We had to wait almost fifteen minutes with engine number three running due to the breakdown of the power plant and until it was replaced by another one, as the B707 had no APU.

While waiting for the power plant to be replaced, the cargo was positioned in the yard. There were exactly eleven pallets, and by my calculations, we should take off at maximum weight. The passenger door was opened and then the main cargo door. A Soviet entered the aircraft with papers containing the weights of each pallet, which were received by Flight Engineer Paul Levi. The load distribution, weight calculations and balancing of the B707 were done manually, however, there was one change we had not expected: the flight was to go to Tripoli, Libya: Muammar-al-Gaddafi's empire; and I knew we would be in Libya's capital for twelve hours, not for pleasure, but to rest.

The change of destination was more of an Iranian strategy, which is not to say that flights to Libya were not monitored by NATO, and especially by the Americans through their warships and spies in Libyan territory. My Flight Engineer, Paul Levi, was Israeli, ex-Mossad and former bodyguard of the deposed Shah of Iran; all that was left was to take him to Gaddafi's house, hand him over and claim the prize for his head.

The Soviet, who was acting as Master Loader, accepted hot coffee made by Paul Levi when I took the opportunity to ask: "How can I make an international call?"

The Soviet asked: "Is it urgent?"

I shook my head positively and with a "yes" in Russian.

The jeep driver took me into a room and pointed to the phone and under the clear glass covering the table, there were area codes and how to make a local and international call. I dialled the numbers calmly but apprehensively when the ringing sound started I counted each one and on completing exactly thirteen the Iranian's voice came from the other end; to me, it was a relief. I explained the situation straightforwardly. Of course, the call was being recorded. As usual, he listened attentively and said: "Consider this matter settled. No one will touch a hair on Paul Levi's head, you have my word. May Allah be with you." And he hung up.

I went back to the aircraft and even more worried. When I reached the galley section I found Paul Levi talking to the other crew members. He looked at me and asked: "Did you manage to resolve my situation?"

And coldly, I replied: "Of course! It's all sorted out." At least so I hoped.

The loading and refuelling went very smoothly and within an hour and five minutes, we were ready for departure. When I looked at the take-off bugs I realised they were high speeds; it meant we were heavy, beyond what was allowed. Three tonnes over the maximum take-off weight. Bones of the trade!

Commander Brooks was in charge of the take-off. He did not question me about the excess weight but gave a briefing alerting me to the fact: The Black Corsair raced down the runway, eager to fly. Brooks pulled the stick to himself beyond the optimum point, the B707 slowly lifted its nose. Then we heard João Guedes' voice: "Positive Rate of Climb," then Brooks' order: "Gear Up," and Paul Levi's alert: "Loss of hydraulic system, loss of hydraulic system."

Heavy aircraft and with loss of hydraulics, but with the

engines running and climbing we were not in serious trouble! Obviously, there was work to be done, although we were mercenaries, it didn't mean we didn't follow the check-list and the manufacturer's general operations manual. That breakdown was an emergency like any other. Commander Brooks kept the B707 at five thousand feet in holding. The weather conditions in Baku were favourable for landing and due to this factor he requested a fuel dump area for the aircraft to land at or near-maximum landing weight, then declared an emergency and commented on the need for time to dump the excess fuel, and manually lowered all three landing gears and blocked the nose gear with the Johnson Bar, which was located in the compartment below the cockpit.

I followed everything without interfering, as the flight commander was John Brooks. At that moment something very important must prevail; what they call nowadays: "cabin coordination" and "decisions by mutual agreement". Some had their flight certificates and licenses still up to date, as well as medical examinations, but most of the crew carried certificates and licenses forged in countries where the Iranian could get "facilities" in exchange for bribe payments.

Two Soviet Mig-25 fighter planes stood in escorts and levelled off. I alerted Commander Brooks to warn the Soviet pilots to stand down before starting the fuel dump. He gave the positive sign as a thank you.

After the fuel dumping procedure, it was time to manually lower the landing gear one by one and lock it in place. My trusty African mechanic Babu helped Paul Levi with the crank, while João Guedes confirmed the landing gear lights and the lock. Paul Levi went to the compartment below the cockpit floor to lock the nose landing gear using the Johnson Bar and returned confirming the mechanical alignment and in cross-check with the respective lamp on the pilot's panel.

When all the check-list was completed and confirmed, Commander Brooks ordered Co-pilot João Guedes to request authorisation for an emergency landing at Baku airport, USSR. I also warned that ADF 1 was unreliable due to the main landing gear doors remaining down and interfering with the ADF reception, as well as drawing attention to the structural speed limitation on approach for landing due to the main landing gear doors being down.

I have always considered that there are lucky men and there are unlucky ones. I was always included in the first condition, but Brooks and João Guedes were not on the lucky list. The approach and landing proceeded naturally with the B707 stopping a few meters from the end of the headland opposite to the landing headland. Commander Brooks noticed that there was no hydraulic steering action and so a tugboat had to intervene. The runway remained closed for almost twenty minutes. I observed everything, but without interfering.

When I arrived at the yard, my faithful African friend Babu went down access 41 to check where the hydraulic loss had occurred. In my experience, the hydraulic leak occurred in one of the landing gear lines when it was commanded. Before long, when Babu confirmed my suspicion. Luckily in the rear hold of the B707, there was a flight kit with repair material, plus two boxes of hydraulic oil each containing twenty-four one-litre cans.

Babu finished the maintenance work in fifty minutes while they refuelled with fuel, which of course went to the Iranian's account. The crew members were already showing fatigue, something dangerous in aviation, whatever it may be.

I asked Commander Brooks for permission to execute the

new take-off, so he could rest. He accepted without complaint, and we took turns during the flight to Tripoli. The take-off went well, and when we reached FL290 I remained in command for an hour and a half; as we levelled off I ordered João Guedes and Babu to go to sleep as well and they both followed my orders, but not before Babu had brought Paul Levi and me some hot coffee without sugar. The two of us remained in the cockpit, apart from the attached autopilot, which allowed us to chat to dispel our tiredness. We were allowed to perform a step climb to FL310, and within minutes we levelled off.

When I left the cockpit my men were fast asleep and it made me return, but Paul Levi had not rested and I ordered him to sit in the co-pilot's seat to get some sleep. I remained in the position of flight engineer and with navigation in hand. Sometimes I would respond to a VHF contact from one of the flight controllers, as well as adjust the bow, and check where we were while keeping track of the weather radar and fuel consumption.

When I flew over Cairo, Egypt, I was authorised to perform another step climb to FL330 with Tripoli bow. Then Commander John Brooks entered the cockpit and took up position in the left-hand seat, with a mug of hot coffee and a ham and cheese sandwich. I relayed the flight guidelines to him. Paul Levi woke up and went to the bathroom to wash his face. My men were back at work and in a few minutes, everyone was in their positions. Then it was my turn to rest. Leaving the cockpit, I found Babu eating a sandwich and drinking Coke.

As we descended, I woke up from the pressurisation effect and followed the whole procedure until landing in Tripoli. Paul Levi's situation worried me, but I hoped that everything would be as the Iranian had said. Two Mig-23 fighters from the Libyan air force were escorting the B707, which followed the Soviet pattern. João Guedes landed safely and, after clearing the runway at the last intersection, Commander John Brooks resumed command and taxied to the patio designated by the follow-me car.

The number of Libyan fighter planes and helicopters was enviable, of various models and manufacturers. Babu's eyes twinkled at the sight of them. The following thought crossed my mind: "This African must already be thinking about how to steal a helicopter from Gaddafi. Don't let him come up with one of those crazy ideas."

At that time, messing with Gaddafi was asking to die. Before we disembarked, I ordered my men to be discreet, to speak a few words, to look at anyone who asked them a question in the face and to be extremely polite. We were taken for document checks in a section for crew members only. I stood next to Paul Levi until he was called by the border agent. Gaddafi's photographs were everywhere we went.

The border agent asked for Paul Levi's passport and proceeded to check it; he looked at it several times and gave the passport back to the Israeli with no questions asked. I was the last to be checked and joined the others as we boarded a bus from the Al Waddan Hotel that was waiting for us. The cargo for Tripoli originating in Baku, USSR, was military. It remained for me to find out what the cargo to the "Base of Operations" was or what was behind that flight.

Something alerted me: any flight scheduled to carry our cargo could suffer a change in the return route. I had to be extra careful not to unload our cargo at an intermediate airport, as the consequences would be the loss of cargo and investments and being discovered by the Iranian. Let us say that he became aware of the transaction while we were resting in a hotel. To be more precise, in a hotel in Tripoli. The differences between the outlaws are outweighed by business interests, but the Iranian was a dealer with no flags and a "friend" of Gaddafi.

A prison is not a pleasant place; and certainly not in Tripoli, incidentally the perfect place to eliminate a competitor. I was not comfortable with Paul Levi's easy entry into Libyan territory, since I was unaware of his real intentions, but the Iranian did not know that Paul Levi was scheduled on that flight until my phone call from Baku. In my view, someone could have informed him.

The Al Waddan Hotel was one of the oldest in Tripoli and comfortable by Arab standards at the time. Honestly, I required a shower with hot water, clean towels and a bed. The hotel room had all these basic items, and I put myself to sleep. I confess it was over eight hours of sleep and disconnected from the world. Until the phone in the room woke me up.

I answered the phone. It was the Iranian. And as usual, he began his sentences with references to Allah as a complement. After the praise-laden sentences came the subject he wanted to address. The Baku cargo to be landed in Tripoli was partial and the other part would go to the "Base of Operations". However, a shipment of state-of-the-art machinery coming from Belgium for high-value mining was to be shipped and I was to accept it without it being on the cargo manifest, only for the weight and balance calculations.

I have always had a privileged mind. I immediately linked the matter to the diamond mining company where Babu's grandfather and father worked in Boma, Zaire, but I did not manifest anything to the Iranian. He gave a detailed account: starting from the embarkation in Belgium by a merchant ship, with a stopover in Lisbon, Portugal, and having as destination Casablanca, Morocco. But, believe me, Morocco was not the final destination; and that did not matter to me at that moment. The machinery meant that the deposit remained with high extraction of the best diamonds in Africa and much purer than those in the Dutch mines in South Africa. It is as I have always said: "Luck always smiles on some. I am one of them."

The adrenaline in my body coursed through my blood and the excitement was very high, almost euphoric, but I realised that I should not put emotions ahead of reason. I needed to keep everything under control and restrain myself to plan every step thoroughly.

The Iranian confessed that the customer had offered a good price for the transfer of the goods and asked me to be very careful since he did not insure the cargo, much less the undeclared cargo. On the other hand, I asked him: "Will we receive any profit from this undeclared cargo?"

He replied with a certain cynicism: "That is not part of the agreement. You know that I'm bowing to a lot of expenses. Remember that the salaries are up to date. Allah will always help us."

I replied: "I have no doubt." Where have you seen someone accept insurance for a phantom aircraft and an undeclared cargo?

It was still early morning when I was awakened by the sound of the telephone and this time by a voice in English laden with a Libyan accent. The reception attendant told me that in forty-five minutes a car would transport us to the airport. I had no choice but to comply. I warned the other crew members and we gathered in the hotel lobby to await transport.

When we arrived at the aircraft, all the cargo was available in the yard next to the B707. I called Paul Levi in for a private chat to explain the machinery. He made no objections or comments, he seemed to know all about it, but the important thing at that moment was to leave, as he wanted to know about the DC8 flight back from Prague with our cargo. After all, the Iranian's profits were guaranteed in his bank account. He negotiated like the Americans: "First show the money."

The commander of the flight was John Brooks. When everything was ready, they decided to start engine number three as a normal sequence; even so, they were unable to do so because the engine would not light up. That malfunction indicated failure of the selected ignition system. The crew switched to system B and still engine number three did not light. My loyal African friend Babu went down access 41 and opened the engine. He had to enlist the help of Paul Levi to remove the cowlings and check the ignition system. Babu removed the spark plugs from the A and B system: both were deteriorated, and once again the flight kit allowed them to be replaced. The engine started successfully, as did the other engines. That is when you realise who is lucky and who is not.

Commander Brooks landed on the "Base of Operations" runway, but by a "misfortune" tyre number four of the right landing gear exploded as it touched the runway. The total of technical problems from the same operating crew was always a "cross" to bear for them. Bad luck surrounded the two pilots. The B707 had to be unloaded on the runway to avoid structural damage and only then was the tyre replaced.

The DC8 returned from Prague and our cargo was duly stored in the hangar under Kruger's guidance. The two Czech structural mechanics were working on the best accessible areas of the Hercules. They decided to postpone the more complex repairs and carry them out after finishing the simpler ones. The next day Tousset arrived in the morning with a truck to remove the machinery and transport it to the end customer. The loader and the men he brought loaded the truck and set off. Before leaving, Tousset came to me and said: "The boss is happy with you, never upset him. He likes you and admires you." He walked away after squeezing mine.

However, to him: "That machinery is sophisticated and expensive. Whoever bought it knew what he was getting. May I know where it is going?"

Tousset replied without any embarrassment: "Boma. Do you know where it is? North-west of the Congo River."

Chapter 5.

The Iranian cargo from Prague and the partial one from Tripoli were dispatched to his clients on more than one flight; due to the fact that the Hercules was in the hangar undergoing maintenance repairs. One of the flights was to Bangassou, the Central African Republic. The landing of the B737 would be on a makeshift dirt airstrip one thousand three hundred metres long. They would unload four pallets of Soviet armament with plenty of ammunition. I assigned to this mission: Commander Douglas, Co-pilot Joseph Marcos and, as Loader Master, Alan Palmer.

Douglas' account was this: on sighting the runway they began the visual approach with progressive descent and departure, with a softer rate of descent due to the runway being shorter than promised, something that was becoming routine. When the B737 was one nautical mile from the landing headland, several shots were fired at the aircraft from the right side. Douglas wasted no time and immediately jumped away, climbing with as much attitude as possible. What occurred in the surroundings of the "landing strip" was the confrontation between government troops and one of the opposing groups for almost fifty minutes, with shots of various calibres. A government helicopter was shot down by a missile.

The government troops were only able to clear the opposing fighter group when two military aircraft began machine-gunning and bombing the enemy positions. Douglas remained in holding at ten thousand feet. One of the military aircrafts made contact and ordered him to maintain that altitude and await directions to land. That armament was a priority for the government troops due to the successful attacks by the opposing group, which cut the supply lines of men, ammunition and supplies. Douglas' lead time was limited due to the amount of fuel. He was to manage it in order to return to the "Base of Operations". However, with three minutes left to abandon the position and return, Douglas was ordered to land by one of the military pilots. All flights to these "uncertain destinations" resulted in suicidal adventures. It was a real Russian roulette. We knew the risks; we were not commercial aviation pilots, but definitely mercenaries of the air.

I remember that during the Vietnam War a detachment of civilian pilots operated under the Air American flag, with support from the CIA and the US army. We never had the support, intelligence logistics and military support like those US pilots. What I knew was that the Iranian maintained a network of contacts with the highest echelons of African governments serving whoever paid the most for the merchandise. He was not interested in ideology, principles or what the final objective and destiny were, but it was up to us to accomplish each mission. The life of a mercenary is worth nothing to a merchant of death or a lord of weapons.

Douglas landed the B737. At the end of the "runway", there were more than two hundred and fifty men, who, on seeing the plane, approached and fired upwards as a show of celebration. Among the heavily armed men: teenagers and children. Each with his inseparable AK-47, according to the account of Co-pilot Joseph Marcos.

Removing the boxes with weapons, ammunition and other supplies was to those men like unloading a truck of ordinary goods. In less than twenty-five minutes Marcos had the main cargo door closed and locked, while Douglas started engine number two. They stated that the take-off was successful, nevertheless, a pressurisation system malfunction limited the flight altitude back to "Base of Operations".

Commander Douglas landed the B737 in the early evening, and only the other day did I see the damage to the airframe. The Czech mechanics were faced with fifteen projectile holes to repair as quickly as possible.

I gathered the two Czech mechanics and Babu in the "Administration House" and got straight to the point: "I need the B737 ready today." The younger one twisted his mouth as if what I demanded was impossible. Once again I repeated: "I need the B737 ready today."

The older and more experienced one said: "The plane will be ready today." They went out the door with Babu, who accompanied them to the hangar, taking Tatus and Mabetu with him to help with the work. What I saw impressed me. At 19:10 that day the B737 was ready for a new mission.

The B737 was loaded to full capacity in the main compartment, plus the holds were crammed with crates of our ordnance and enough fuel for Freetown, Sierra Leone. My men were waiting to see who would be called up for another adventure and at nine-thirty p.m. I announced the name of Co-pilot Igor Kracoviv, the Romanian, Babu and myself.

The B737 took off at five-thirty a.m. the next day. Before leaving, I talked to Kauffman to accompany the repairs to the Hercules, as the deliveries were delayed and as soon as it was ready, they should load it with full load for Lagos, Nigeria. Those assigned were Commander Lee, Co-pilot Jean-Batiste, Flight Engineer Velasquez, Master Loader and Mechanic Mabetu.

Kruger coordinated all the contacts of the smuggling of our cargo. The investments started to gain financial volume. The German knew with whom to negotiate, and up to the moment what was agreed with the suppliers was fulfilled and to demonstrate the capacity to honour the payments, something that became a "credit card", without the flag of the financiers and banks.

The approach procedure of the B737 to Freetown, Sierra Leone, was carried out by Co-pilot Igor Kracoviv flying over the sea. Freetown control cleared him to descend to four thousand feet and, after reaching FL040, he remained at that flight level for two minutes and continued the descent for landing. The B737 was proceeding to the intersection of the Localiser when Igor Kracoviv initiated the turn to finally close it and meet the runway axis with Flap 25°. On intercepting the Localiser, he ordered: Landing Gear Down, and confirmed landing gear lowered and locked. The B737 intercepted Glide Slope, maintaining descent rate at three hundred feet per minute with final approach speed compatible with landing weight. At one thousand feet altitude it suddenly sounded engine fire alarm number two. Igor Kracoviv, in an unexpected reaction, decided to go around with B737-200 Adv.

There was no time for "debates". I took Igor's command with the phrase "I have control!" and proceeded to land. After silencing the sound of the fire alarm, however, the lamp on the number two engine fire-extinguishing command handle remained lit and I ordered Full Flap Down and I landed the B737 in complete safety.

The Romanian was disconcerted but not irritated; that was a good sign. Freetown airport had a basic structure that made the mission easier. During the taxi, we were intercepted by a vehicle with armed men who signalled us to follow them. During the taxi, I switched on the APU to ensure electrical power and pneumatic pressure for the next departure.

I switched off the engines and asked Babu to open the cowlings of engine number two and check the fire detection sensors. When Babu left the cockpit I explained to Igor why I had taken over from him: "In final, configured for landing, when the fire alarm sounds and landing is assured, you do not go-around. It is better to land and fight the fire on the ground than to pitch and risk a single-engine landing." The Romanian calmly accepted my decision. However, men's egos are hit and this leaves a silent hurt inside. Only those who see that there is always something to learn dilute these silent hurts, and the result for an airman is to become an ace.

My faithful African friend Babu opened the cowlings of engine number two and kept them that way for checks while the refuelling truck connected the hoses at the fuel station. The Romanian remained in the cockpit to insert the navigation back, while some curious people approached the open engine, but Babu asked them to stay away.

I was on the ground and at that moment a black gentleman with white hair approached and said to me: "The birds are smaller here."

I replied: "Just like everywhere else in Africa". That phrase meant that everything was ready to unload our cargo. The white-haired gentleman escorted me into the galley of the B737 with a nylon bag. I asked him to go into the cockpit and open the bag.

He obeyed and said: "It's all there."

After inspection, Babu went to the cockpit and said: "Captain, everything is in perfect condition. May I close the engine cowlings?"

I permitted him, and he went to accompany the fuel refuelling. Before leaving the cockpit, I asked him to bring a mug of hot coffee, accompanied by a glass of water. Then I asked him to close the cockpit door. I immediately locked it, avoiding any intruders. I was drinking my coffee when the Romanian, without looking at me, asked: "The fire alarm was false. Wasn't it?" I continued drinking the coffee and waited a few seconds. With anxiety for an answer, he asked the question once again.

I replied: "The fire alarm was false and what I explained to you is a fact. Are we clear?"

The Romanian was responsible for taking off from Freetown and landing at the "Base of Operations". I took the opportunity to get some sleep during the trip. Neither during take-off nor landing did the "fire alarm sound again". The nylon bag contained four hundred and seventy-five thousand US dollars. The business was booming and there was still a lot of money available to be earned, yet what he had in mind was a "definitive mission", never to return to that life in which every second could be his last.

When one accumulates a large sum of money one must be very careful with ambitious people and traitors. The total amount already exceeded the first million dollars; of course, the per capita value would not solve any one's life. There were two ways out of this equation: the first was to continue their missions, risking their lives, exposing themselves to all kinds of luck and surviving with part of the booty. The second, to plan something big that would free us once and for all from that life. However, there was something they loved and it was in their blood: being mercenary pilots.

I took care to buy more modern weaponry for my men and did not skimp on Belgian machine guns, German pistols, bladed weapons and suitable clothing. The two Czech mechanics Gustav and Nikolij joined the group after a direct conversation and quickly learnt that silence had the price of gold.

My faithful African friend Akin warned that once again the "Base of Operations" could be the target of a new attack and in greater proportions. I did not have enough men to face for long the troops of fighters willing to do anything. What made their leaders avoid us was the fact that we were mercenaries and the presence of the "bad man" who lived on the African savannah. We were aviators who demonstrated the capacity to face them, but our flying activities drew attention because of the movement of large jets at any time of the day or night.

There is, among scholars of Machiavelli, the Wise, a much-discussed and present concept in international relations: "Before you attack me, I do it first and preferably eliminate you."

I asked Akin: "Do you have any way of knowing where these men are hiding?"

He replied in all simplicity and coolness: "I don't know today, but tomorrow I will."

My faithful African friend Akin hired a tracker from one of the nearby villages. I agreed to the price the man asked to do the job. Within three days I knew: where they were, how many there were, the type of weaponry and the power of defence. No doubt they were many and of remarkable operational fragility. So, I organised what I might call "a hunt". I gathered my men together and explained what was coming and as their leader, I was not willing to give an inch of what we conquered.

They listened carefully to the plan of action and how to execute it; that would be the ultimate test of confidence in the leadership I exercised. Our vehicles were prepared with machine guns, thirty-millimetre calibre, ammunition sufficient for five days' combat, medium and high detonation explosives, fragmentation grenades, pistols and high-tech machine guns with grenade launchers.

We arrived at the area early in the morning, where there were approximately fifty-two men, and we surrounded the place to the point of not letting any one leave alive. Luckily for us, there were no children in this group of fighters and it was not my place to rate them ideally. They were a potential threat, there was no chance of negotiation: "Peace treaties are signed to be torn up and end in blood." So why waste time? "Let's get to the bottom of the matter and then there will be no doubt."

We penetrated the area eliminating the sentries by beheading them and went to where the weapons were stored. Then we blew everything up. At that moment, at sunrise, the desperation of the enemy was terrifying: my men shot them down without mercy. A military officer wielded his AK-47 next to a sergeant firing at my battle group. I did not lose my cool; I drew my forty-five calibre pistol and fired hitting the sergeant in the neck, which caused him to spin and drop dead. The military officer spun the AK-47 towards me firing in a desperate sequence to shoot me down; I aimed at the unfortunate man's head and pressed the trigger firmly: his head ricocheted backwards with part of his face blown off.

None of the African combatants survived, and those who still stubbornly made it out alive were executed without remorse. It was the only way to be sure that they would not attack us and would not return, not from the world of the dead. When we returned from that mission to the "Base of Operations" we did it in silence in our vehicles, there was no feeling of victory but of survival, it could be the same way with us. Machiavelli once wrote: "Occupy, dominate and eliminate." Wise man. The story that ran through the African savannah was that there was a bad white man, very bad, to the point of being the Devil himself.

As we arrived back from our trip to Freetown, Sierra Leone, I realised that Hercules was loaded and ready to go. My orders were followed to the letter and this allowed me time to think. This is not to say that I trusted them, no, I never trusted any one, for I know the human essence: "We are born good and we become bad."

Commander Lee passed us with the Hercules in the opposite direction taxiing to the take-off headland. He opened the window and saluted us with his left hand; I reciprocated in the same manner. The flight to Lagos, Nigeria, would be on the same pattern as Freetown, with the Commander bringing the bag with the proceeds of our investments.

The fuel tank for the aircraft was at a quarter of the maximum tank capacity. That was a matter of no concern to me: without fuel, the Iranian would cease to make a profit. It does not cost anything to alert the one who thinks he is the master of my destiny, and after two days five trucks full of fuel aviation entered the "Base of Operations", as well as two trucks with supplies and essential items. Leading the convoy was Tousset.

He handed over a folder with bank documents showing the deposits of each man's wages. He asked: "Does the boss want to know if you still have the money he sent you?"

I looked into Tousset's coal-coloured eyes and said: "Yes, it's with me. Do you want it back now?"

He replied: "No, not at all. The boss wants to know if you still have it with you, that's all."

I was suspicious of that meaningless question and let it pass as if it had no importance. Tousset's visit always meant a report to his boss. I took advantage of the "messenger's" stay and sent a letter in a sealed envelope to the Iranian. In it, I requested two more Hercules as a matter of urgency and a Bell UH-1 helicopter, the same model used in the Vietnam War, in addition to other administrative matters. I even reported on Enrico and without mentioning how the Italian left for hell.

I confess that I was given a significant amount of money in my bank account as a reward for my performance. The Iranian knew how to give meat to the lions, however, I had in my hands more than he could imagine; I do not refer to the financial values but to the human capital, which, day after day, kept him under my control.

I needed to travel to Cape Town, South Africa, to hire the services of private safes and save all the capital acquired without compromising that destined for reinvestment. Then a unique opportunity arose. The Iranian knew that the number two engine on the B737-200 Adv needed to be replaced as it was experiencing high temperatures during take-off and to avoid the worst he hired a maintenance company in Johannesburg, South Africa to replace it. The B737-200 Adv would remain three days in South African territory, and so would I, enough time to take care of business. Luck is a personal matter.

The Hercules was handling the missions and was flying almost every day distributing the Iranian's cargo. I realised that certain crew members were the right measure for international flights, among them: Kauffman, Kruger, Jean-Pierre, Jean-Batiste, João Guedes, Germam Holt, Hans Marzevic, Paul Levi and myself. Sometimes I would call others, depending on my interests in the mission. Other crew members identified themselves with cargo distribution flights, despite the ever-imminent danger, but with all the uncertainties surrounding us, we had no more casualties in that period.

My Czech mechanics would spring into action and sort out the airframe issues. I cannot deny that the patches on the Hercules were many, which meant fuel consumption due to deteriorating flight performances.

I returned to South Africa several times. At that time, I decided to start an import-export company Ltd in Cape Town. In this company, I contributed significant funds of my own, through a bank account, and built up a business and financial relationship with my chosen bank, despite the Apartheid policy that prevailed, although I disagreed with it. I bought a small commercial property as a fixed address, as it was one of the requirements for the process of opening the company, as well as I got a nominated accountant who, over time, became almost a "confidant priest", not to call him Rabbi.

He was Jewish of Dutch origin, married and a collector of antique clocks, but I never visited his house. I imagine all those clocks announcing the time at the same time. He was a competent, methodical and organised man: he only did not work on Saturdays because of the religious issue, which did not concern me. Imagine Paul Levi refusing to work on Saturday. My Jewish accountant's name was Ben-Ami, which means in Hebrew if memory serves me right: "son of his people or son of the people". At least by that name, my accountant was "popular, of the people". However, the price was for the elite; not that I minded, for it was and is worth every penny.

On the trip to South Africa for the engine change of the B737-200 Adv, I did not take Babu with me. I needed him in Zaire, and who accompanied me was Commander Mark Kurt. The night before I travelled, I asked Babu to meet me at the "Administration House". He knew I would be travelling the next day. For some years I kept my faithful African friend close by. I guided Babu to a special mission south of the small town of Boma. The African said goodbye to me and prepared for the trip by using one of the vehicles and taking with him: weapons, money, supplies and whatever else he deemed necessary.

Kruger coordinated all the smuggling operations and accounted for the investments and returns. The accumulation of capital with each mission represented the incentive that everyone desired. When I returned from South Africa I gathered my men together to explain to them the gains we were making. Each one knew how much he had to receive, regardless of the salaries that the Iranian deposited in their bank accounts in the UK. The silence was mandatory when we dealt with this matter. I never had a problem in that regard.

The B737-200 Adv received a new engine and the head of maintenance wanted to talk to me. At first, I thought it was about the service, but he asked: "Who repaired the airframe?"

And to save time I returned with another question: "Why do you want to know?"

He was a little disconcerted and in an even humble way stated: "The repairs were very successful, for the shots it took."

The maintenance chief was a thin, blond man, close to sixty years old and always with a cigarette in his mouth, yet he didn't dare light one of his in front of me. I replied with a certain cynicism: "The important thing now is the repairs, not how it was punctured."

The B737-200 Adv engine change did not require a flight test, only run-up and fine-tuning of power and idle speed, so it was done.

The Iranian could not do anything wrong. I received the aircraft ready to fly, while nine pallets were lined up with cargo, including for the holds. The destination of the armament and ammunition was for northern Angola for the "combatants" against the central government in Luanda. We took off with two tonnes above the maximum take-off weight, and consequently above the maximum landing weight. Still, the B737-200 Adv held up.

The African savannah has always been a great mystery. I'm not a lover of animal life and the landscape has always been a postcard changing colour and hue. Animal life is perfect on that giant and beautiful continent: "Seeing nature in harmony and balance has always been the envy of human beings on this earth."

Two weeks passed of intense work, and my men, and each day they gained confidence and experience. They're always armed, regardless of the activity, because many men, including military men, die under enemy attack because they are unarmed. Paul Levi held this premise, which I defended. It was no accident that the Israeli soldier does not leave his weapon even to go to the bathroom. That week I warned that we would receive two more Hercules and a helicopter. The men shouted for joy, but I did not allow random shooting.

The two Hercules were at the airport in the city of Al-Jawf, Libya, southwest of Gaddafi's country. This mission was to be very well coordinated, it involved transporting the crew to Al-Jawf and back to the "Base of Operations". I had no intention of moving my men to an international airport and following them as tourists. The chances of one of them being identified and detained were almost one hundred per cent. The Iranian did not refuse my decision to move our battered old Hercules to Al-Jawf, Libya. Furthermore, I demanded that our stay in Libyan territory be as short as possible.

We took off at four a.m. with a bow from Al-Jawf and three full crews. The three Hercules would meet different destinations and with cargo on board from Al-Jawf to Niamey in Niger, Morovia in Liberia and Addis Ababa in Ethiopia. I flew the older and beaten Hercules bowing Addis Ababa and carrying the Bell UH-1 helicopter with attack and defence weaponry, which was ready for action. I made sure that the floor had reinforcement with a twin steel plate, intending to prevent the crew from being hit on the attack, but it was a relative defence. Helicopters were never an example of "strong apache". I always preferred fixed wings.

The story of that helicopter was another one of the negotiations the Iranian made with the African leader in exchange for favours and money. Babu was passionate about those flying machines. He was euphoric when he saw and touched the Bell UH-1 and in excellent condition. I have not forgotten what he said: "This time there was no need to steal it." My faithful African friend showed in his eyes the joy of a child when he receives a present on Kings Day. In my opinion, more pilots would be needed, but that would depend a lot on international flights, and for those flights, we only had the B707 and the DC8.

When a group of men are under the intense pressure of daily life, there is no room for thoughts to take them out of focus; but it is idleness that allows the Devil to occupy the mind. I kept up an intense work regime, apart from piloting, with all sorts of tasks: from peeling potatoes to repairing a gearbox on a turboprop engine. This was by way of example, as there were much more complex jobs.

The tactic was to keep them active: "Those who don't know learn, those who know teach." And it worked perfectly, as well as producing a bond of friendship, despite not having the pretensions of creating an "educational school", but of keeping minds busy.

If there is one thing that almost all men like, it is women, and my men, besides enjoying a good beer and whisky, were women, lovers. I was planning a recreational trip for them to a women's brothel, the bill would be for the Iranian. In the account book, I registered it as "recreation" because their boss was averse to this worldly promiscuity, however, having three women as wife according to his customs and religion was something: normal. And why would a brothel of women not be normal for my men?

The three Hercules departed crammed with pallets full of crates containing armaments and ammunition. I sometimes thought that the peoples of Africa would rise up on a war footing against the world and invade every continent. Of course, it was an absurd idea! Where were all these armaments and ammunition going? I learned in time that: for every ten projectiles fired by Africans, only one had a combat purpose. Ninety per cent was wasted and the cost was high, yet for the warlords, they formed an unparalleled clientele.

Part of the armament that arrived in West Africa was "exported" to Latin America through Paraguay, however, the Soviet rifles still suffered some resistance to enter some countries such as Brazil and Argentina, despite this, drug traffickers, remaining guerrilla groups and other insurgent groups became interested in this model of rifle. The orders increased to the point that China participated in the business with the production of the copy of the Soviet assault rifle.

The differences between the rifles were significant: the Chinese copy did not allow the coupling of grenade launchers and silencers, besides having a fixed bayonet. The price, compared to the Belgian, British, French, German and Israeli models, was a trifle, not to mention versatile in all terrains and low maintenance costs. Nobody manufactures and trades AK-47s to hunts birds!

The North Vietnamese troops, in combat against South Vietnam and its North American allies, showed the unique sound of an AK-47 in action and its combat efficiency. South American guerrillas use it to this day as a combat rifle. The arms shops in the United States sell them to citizens in a democratic way, whether the Chinese or Soviet model, as do the traffickers in Mexico, Colombia, Peru, Bolivia and Brazil. The market is vast and the clientele diverse with a single objective: to pull the trigger, some in the name of freedom, others in the name of their cartels. I became part of the intermediation and only wanted a fat slice of the trigger-happy cake.

The three Hercules arrived at the "Base of Operations" on the same day, but with a small-time difference. The yard was previously prepared to receive the two new members of the fleet and christen them in their fuselages. One of them was named "Eagle from the Desert" and the other "Mikimba Warrior", in honour of the late African mechanic. Czech mechanics inspected the structure and concluded that the only way to improve them was if they were new from the factory. And believe me: those Hercules belonged to the fleet of one of the UN Security Council countries. Draw your own conclusions.

Babu handed me a complete report of the mission I had assigned him in Boma. I would study the contents later. On arriving from Addis Ababa, I ordered my men to rest for twenty-four hours. It was in that interval that I decided to read with full attention what Babu had to inform me. Near the "Administration House" there were two trees nearby that allowed me to tie a good hammock under excellent shade. With time I adapted some particular comforts, but without privileges.

I read the precise and meticulous report very carefully, which allowed me to think up an audacious plan that included every man under my command; but as my grandmother used to say: "Hot soup is eaten by the edges."

The armed conflicts between Africans: between coups d'état, tribal and ideological disputes, kept a good part of our missions going and our illicit enrichment since there were always soldiers with "plenty of money leftover" and with a sure destination. Look at this curiosity: we took care that our cargo was illegally loaded on an illegal flight with illegal Iranian cargo. It was perfect!

The criminals of the smuggling world also mediated negotiations, and sometimes there was an excess of supply for the same product. Kruger always consulted me and the answer was: "No new partners, only known ones, because there is a high possibility of infiltration by Interpol police."

Not to be unfair to Interpol: one of Kruger's contacts was arrested in Brussels, Belgium. That supplier was reliable, but after two days he was released and hit the streets. I learned about it in Africa and decided to eliminate the "big mouth". My origin is French and Italian: on the Italian side is the quiet Comune di Maratea, to the south. There I have some *amici*, almost all of them members of the Cosa Nostra, but a request at this level was not common and nothing like a good price for full service. I travelled to Rome on a commercial flight and in possession of my Italian passport; I don't deny that I had several passports of different nationalities and false ones, but that doesn't mean that the Italian passport was.

At that time airports were less "complicated" but basic services worked. I looked for a phone booth outside Rome airport

121

and called Giussepe Schinini, a great friend, and asked to speak to Don Antonino in Palermo, Sicily. He wanted to know personally the reason and invited me to meet him in Maratea.

Earlier that same evening; Giussepe and I had dinner in a restaurant of the *famiglia*. He was a burly man and taller than me. Among some of the questions he asked, he wanted to know what I did for a living, which is like saying what my line of business was. If you want their trust there are simple and strict rules to be followed. One of them is respect and speaking the truth; it doesn't mean that you have to give an account of your life, because they are immediately suspicious: "He who talks too much ends up eating grass by the roots."

Giussepe arranged the meeting with Don Antonino and I travelled to Palermo. I was not a member of the Cosa Nostra, my request to a powerful Italian Mafia boss did not interfere in his business. I had an offer to make, besides the price on the head of the Kruger contact. I confess that Don Antonino's house impressed me by the splendid view, manicured gardens, imposing and cinematic entrance to his mansion. I was met by the security men and thoroughly searched despite the recommendations of my friend from Maratea, and then asked to wait in a large office well laid out and comfortable. I sat facing a splendid open window that allowed me to see an unparalleled view of the sea. The main door remained open and with the full attention of the security guards. It didn't bother me at all. I would probably do the same.

Don Antonino entered the office accompanied by another man. The Mafia boss was gentle and polite. No displays of power. And as time passed and conversations took place, I learned that the man accompanying him was his *consiglieri*. He was the one who analysed the "visitor's" request, but the final word was Don Antonino's. I've always been lucky, and that day was no different. We agreed on a payment amount and a minimum percentage of participation in the profits of the African operations since there would be no "investment" on his part.

I learned a lot with Don Antonino. The most important was the respect that he always maintained with me, besides the reciprocity between two criminals, mainly in the fulfilment of *il nostro accordo* financier. With this my access to other matters passed to a status of singular importance. I did not forget Giussepe, and, with Don Antonino's permission, I gratified my *amico* of Maratea. And make no mistake that a percentage ended up in the hands of Don Antonino, of that I have no doubt.

Don Antonino knew that there was urgency in my request and ordered his *consiglieri* to provide everything and in an "impeccable" way, besides wanting to receive for the head of that unfortunate Belgian. From my suitcase, I took half the agreed amount and placed it on the table. There, they realised that I was not anybody. The Belgian contact was executed three days after my business visit. I learned much later that the deceased was part of the structure of a building then under construction, this from the mouth of Don Antonino's *consiglieri*.

Back to my business, I decided to stay in a hotel for one night in Rome. What was the point of going back to hell with such trepidation? I chose the Luxury Le Grand Hotel, with a room facing the street, and after a long hot shower, I slept soundly. In the early evening, I woke up and had another bath, got dressed, went to the hotel restaurant and had a meal of typical Italian cuisine that I had not tasted for a long time: beef, potatoes, asparagus and rice with sultanas and chestnuts, accompanied by wine from the Tuscany region. I could not leave Rome without another stroke of luck.

I was drinking coffee when a young woman dressed in her Alitalia Airways stewardess uniform arrived at the hotel. She caught my eye for her well-drawn body, her hair that matched her light brown eyes and Venus lips. The gods of Olympus had sent her to tempt me into Paradise. She was sin in the body of Aphrodite, and I was not Apollo and have never been daring with women; I think shyness has always been a hindrance since adolescence, however, understand no one is saved from destiny! When I finished dinner I went to the hotel reception and she had disappeared, the same way she arrived from Olympus without warning.

I went up the lift to the floor where I was staying and was walking towards my room when I saw her for the second time trying to open the door to my room. I made no noise and approached very carefully as this beautiful woman tried to open the door without success. Without scaring her, I held her hand for the first time. I inserted my key into the lock and opened the door. Surprisingly, she was not confused as she looked at the key number, she smiled making out that she had got the wrong room. I never knew why she did it. I didn't ask. Still, she with a beautiful smile and in an almost juvenile voice asked in English for me to enter too.

I remained to wait outside without her realising the mistake she was making: my bed was messy and with my personal hygiene belongings scattered about. It was me who had not understood the inexplicable.

I confess that it was one of the most intense nights I have had with a woman. We talked as if we had known each other for a long time; I was nevertheless attentive to the fact that she carried a large sum of money, as well as being charming, not to say seductive. She was far from being a nun. Our affair went far beyond the time I imagined, for our affair lasted until she decided to marry a Commander of the airline where she worked. She knew my life was furtive and that I was not a man on a schedule to get home punctually.

It was no surprise to me the marriage was for the best for her. In the depths of my unfeeling heart, I was happy, however, fate is merciless: three months into the marriage she died in a car accident while driving from Zurich to Milan.

In short: I was not a widower. As one of my lawyers says: "Life goes on"; at least my life since I could have been in the Aston Martin she was driving. I learned a year and a half later that she was having an affair with a Swiss banker. Of course, I obviously would not have been in the Aston Martin that day.

When I returned to Kinshasa by commercial flight, my faithful African friend Babu was waiting for me at the airport exit. On the way to the "Base of Operations" he filled me in on everything and what caught my attention was the number of flights to Gaddafi's Libya, in addition to the schedule of international flights, as it was these flights that brought our cargo.

Through Tousset I managed to install two more telephone lines. And for the first time, it was possible with my own investments to buy two computers, a fax machine and an internet service. I had never seen anything so primitive; and for that time, we were "light years" ahead, despite the operational limitations of the system, the distance from the provider and the stability of the services. I learned about the new telecommunication technology from a British magazine while passing through Rome airport.

The isolation of the African savannah almost takes us back to the "cave era". Away from the world of technology, newspapers, news, economy and facts. That technology opened "windows", and I realised that my accumulated capital had found one of the destinations for the future: world telecommunications, what came to be known as the "telecommunications network". Nevertheless, I did not want partners, I never trusted partners: "The best partner is yourself."

To participate in business decisions, it is necessary to "be present". It does not mean to be physically present, but to penetrate the business world as a great speculator, the level of capital contribution is essential; as well as knowing the rules of the game. And nothing better than The Zurich Axioms as the teaching basis of the speculation game and The Prince as the lethal weapon. There are no angels in business. As my grandfather used to say: "Where there is money, there are no scruples." Wrong. "Where there is money, there is more money."

What is the function of a bank? I answer: "To sell money." The bank only needs idiots to buy it. My capital accumulated month by month, despite the high risk, to get it. And it was worth every penny.

Libya had the largest arms depots in North Africa. The number of armaments and ammunition exceeded the calculations of any intelligence agency, and remember ammunition was made to be used, and for Gaddafi, it was imperative to get rid of excess "old" ammunition. The price to pass it on was a trifle and a fortune was being made. What did Gaddafi get for renewing the deposits with new ammunition? Money, a lot of money in personalised and secret accounts abroad, because he prioritised the purchase to his main supplier: the Iranian. How did I get access to this information? I can answer through Paul Levi because the Israeli ex-Mossad sometimes "talked the talk".

The Iranian was interested in selling new weapons and ammunition to Gaddafi due to the value of the operations, but I thought long and hard before "interfering" in other people's business. The only way would be to bribe whoever was the "guardian" of the deposits.

Even so, if this "gatekeeper" was discovered I can't imagine what the maximum penalty would be for the traitor. Bribery is not difficult.

I have made many trips to Libya flying Hercules and carrying all kinds of cargo, including "dangerous cargo". Our stay in Libya facilitated contact with the people who dealt directly with ammunition. On one of these trips, Commander Douglas was approached by a Libyan military officer who expressed interest in selling "old" ammunition. Have no doubt that I was suspicious, even so, listening to an offer does not mean accepting it.

Commander Douglas waited for me to arrive from one of the flights to Damascus, Syria, and reported what had happened. As I said before: "luck is not for everyone." I left for Libya on the next scheduled flight in one of the Hercules, with Commander John Brooks, Co-pilot Joseph Marcos, Flight Engineer Alan Palmer and Master Loader and mechanic Tatus. I bet the military man would go to the Hercules hoping to find someone to negotiate with, as Douglas told him he was not the one doing the negotiating, but he bet the military man a thousand dollars if I would not be among one of the next flights for a negotiation. Douglas bet well and received for the wager. I liked his daring. In a way, he was bold to believe there was a good chance of business. That is not to say that he knew the real risks; I mean those hidden to the eyes of many and quite clear to others.

Before setting off for Libya, I sought out Paul Levi and asked his opinion. Israelis, when they come into the world, are already born suspicious of their own shadow. His words were these: "It is dangerous. You don't know who you are and what you might unleash. I don't recommend negotiating with terrorists." I have always distrusted the Israelis; besides, in business, there is no such thing as terrorists: money is always money!

The Hercules parked near the cargo already predestined for the aircraft, and after chocking the main wheels, John Brooks ordered the main rear cargo door unlocked and lowered to allow for the planned loading. The Master Loader Tatus complied with the orders, returned to the cockpit and said: "Captain, there is a Libyan military waiting for someone and near the cargo door." John Brooks did not know what this was about. I ordered them to maintain activities and withdrew from the cockpit, going to meet the Libyan serviceman. When I reached the rear door he was looking at the drift of the Hercules, as if searching for something. I'll not reveal the name of the Libyan military, who is alive today and resides in Paris.

He was cordial and objective and got straight to the point. Then I asked the price of the "product" and I was surprised because the only demand he made was to buy the whole lot that was under his responsibility. The warehouse contained ninety tons of "old" ammunition for AK-47s, which represented approximately eleven million two hundred and fifty thousand rounds. His asking price was three million three hundred and seventy-five thousand dollars. It was an excellent deal for me. I offered as a final bid two million two hundred and fifty thousand dollars, which is like saying that each projectile would cost twenty cents on the dollar. The resale of the same lot would be seventy-five cents on the dollar, an estimated net profit of five million six hundred and twenty-five thousand dollars, not including the cost of transport for the "new owner".

So far these were words in the wind, besides having to organise the logistics of transport and storage of ninety tonnes of ammunition in Zaire, and before travelling to Libya, and after talking to Paul Levi, I sought out Kruger and questioned him about us buying a load of "old" ammunition. What I wanted to know was who would buy it immediately, and my smuggling negotiator said: "The Latin American guerrillas because they have funding from narcotraffickers." I ordered Kruger to offer a shipment of "old" ammunition, but to warn those interested that the ammunition was well stored and free of moisture.

We left for Libya in the early afternoon. Kruger got a response a week and a half after meeting in Libya with the military officer. The ammunition had two destinations: Colombia and Brazil. The merchandise was to enter through Asunción, Paraguay, and for that Kruger had to bribe the police's top brass. The first problem I had to solve was finding an aircraft capable of carrying ninety tonnes of cargo in a single flight. I ruled out transport by air and decided to opt for the sea route, using the exit via the Congo River, Zaire, and the contracted ship gaining bow at Asunción.

I ordered to start the mission to withdraw the ammunition from Libya when fifty per cent of the payment was guaranteed in my company's bank account in Cape Town. The deposit was made through a bank in the Cayman Islands by a businessman who dealt in large sums of money and foreign exchange. Everything ran with full bank secrecy and the guarantees provided. After all my company was one of exports and imports.

When all the ammunition arrived at the "Base of Operations", I hired seven carts capable of transporting the cargo to the Liberian-flagged ship, but the carts were loaded only after confirming the deposit of the difference in my bank account. The ship left the territorial water of Zaire with the bow of Asunción, which would sail up the Paraguay River, unload, and the cargo would continue to its destination.

My part was to get it to Asunción and from there it was up to the clients. The guerrillas in Colombia received the shipment six days after landing. The client in Brazil was a "businessman" who lived in Brasilia and supplied the traffickers from the slums of Rio de Janeiro, the city and periphery of São Paulo, as well as other places. However, I don't know why he had difficulties with the Brazilian police authorities. It's a matter that doesn't concern me.

The Libyan military made good money from negotiating the ammunition depots. He could have earned more during the negotiations with me, but he preferred to bet enough and withdraw in time. As I stated, he is still living. At that time, my capital had reached the sum of one hundred and sixty-five million US dollars.

My men worked hard, and each had accumulated up to that point more than five million US dollars. I was paying more than any investment in the world of capital markets. If you want your human resources faithful and competent, pay them well!

Chapter 6.

Since the beginning of the missions, seven years had passed and the world was no longer the same with the fall of the Berlin Wall: what was to come was the defeat of a powerful opponent of the USA. The plot that was woven around the USSR was quite clear, and the Soviet military-industrial park would be available to all warlords. Why not go shopping?

The biggest customers for weapons were the countries of Africa, where the conflicts had no time to end. Several countries were very interested in the natural resources that this giant continent offered the world, but at an infinite human cost. Business intensified even more. Aircraft needed overhauls and for the Iranian, it was not essential and a priority. We lived a hard life, with no room for fear, and still wished to enjoy the accumulated capital. During those seven quick years we worked: twelve months in a row each year, we suffered nine attacks from all kinds of armed groups, no doctors and no social life whatsoever, yet there was in each one the hope of returning to their homes and families. Of course, the ones who still had a family to return to.

Late one Friday afternoon we were all at the "Base of Operations". I ordered the men to go to the hangar and there advised that flight operations were suspended until the aircraft was in an operational and safe condition. A question echoed through the hangar: "Why only now? We are used to it," João

Guedes questioned me.

I replied: "Because of our safety. There is no point in swimming, swimming and dying on the beach." Everyone understood my decision. The spare and replacement parts arrived in two carts, opening the way was Tousset, for the Iranian took steps to avoid the worst.

It took a fortnight of hard work to get the aircraft in a more suitable operational condition. After seven straight years, none of us had our flight licences and medical certificates revalidated. To us, they were unnecessary items with the false documents we carried. My men were now disciplined and organised, not for any reason leaving their rifles out of reach. Paul Levi had been instructing them in self-defence and combat for some time. He used the knowledge acquired in the martial art of Israeli origin called: Krav Maga, which proved to be efficient and useful, but not unbeatable.

My men acquired the ideal physical conditions. The only one who was not interested in Paul Levi's instructions was João Guedes; after all, it was not compulsory. Although the environment was different I never trusted anyone, no matter how safe I appeared, I always considered that a mercenary is a mercenary, there are not exceptions. I kept the plan for Boma alive. All conditions were converging to achieve the objectives, despite the time that passed, however, it was imperative to mature and put in place a bold plan, and all that mattered was winning.

Uganda was in the midst of a tribal civil war; the deliveries of arms and ammunition went to high risk. The report of some crew members and the state in which the aircraft was returning to the "Base of Operations" confirmed the real situation. João Guedes was the first to speak out in protest. He preferred flights to Europe or other less risky places. And who wouldn't? There were no heroes! We were no heroes! We were mercenaries. I decided to climb João Guedes on the B707 for flights outside the "risk area". I allowed for the first time, a privilege, which is what lawyers call: "creating a jurisprudence". None of my men protested, but silence is the harbinger of shouting.

I started flying the Hercules instead of the "jurisprudence pilot". I carried out more than twenty missions of the type: "Welcome to the gates of hell", to the point that each time I returned to the "Base of Operations", I was awaited with a certain apprehension by my men, according to the report of some. I started flying a single Hercules, the oldest and most beaten. It was like a "good luck charm". For them, I entered the hall of flying legends, to the point that Kauffman claimed that I was the "Reincarnation of the Red Baron", since, every time I appeared at the door of the Hercules after a mission, and the brave plane more punctured than Swiss cheese, and without a scratch. Everyone believed I was Osiris when arrived on Earth. Understand once and for all! Nothing is free in this life and between the lines: those men would follow me anywhere under my leadership and including Boma.

One of the most told stories by my men to this day: my order was to accomplish the mission, and that regardless of the hostile scenario. The destination of the cargo was Kigali, Rwanda. The Hercules was prepared with two machine guns on the sides, fifty-millimetre calibre, as well as keeping on board four Soviet portable anti-tank launchers, British high fragmentation grenades, our inseparable state-of-the-art Belgian automatic rifles, pistols and knives.

The scenario was the worst possible. The clashes of infantry and armour did not define whose victory that day would be. Columns of black smoke were rising, showing the violence employed between the two sides. Under my command we approached by the northwest sector, which seemed more favourable; when the anti-aircraft batteries began the defence of the sector, I continued the direct descent to the landing strip; the projectiles went up in an insane cadence and under the floor of Commander Mark Kurt's side a projectile crossed between his legs, bursting through the ceiling and without any effect. Another projectile of smaller calibre passed between us and exited the opposite side. The fuselage received an unseen fusillade charge. In front of the nose exploded the anti-aircraft projectiles that made the Hercules shudder, but the gods of Olympus, with their invisible shields, would not let our souls be delivered to the Boatman, even if each of us carried two coins in our pockets, always.

A blunt impact was felt against the fuselage to the point of altering the bow, while Mark Kurt helped me keep the final intersection straight as firmly as possible. Then the number three engine received a deadly shot to the underside, exposing the guts of the brave engine and locking the propeller in place for good. The Hercules shuddered brutally, followed by another that ripped a chunk out of the left side of the fuselage, but we were proceeding to land. When a quarter of a mile away the right wing was sifted with shots and another high-calibre impact hit the rear of the fuselage and almost took us off the final axis for landing. We crossed the headland with the number three engine spewing black smoke but totally isolated, we landed on the runway and applied brakes to try to enter the first intersection when a mortar rushed thirty metres from the Hercules with no apparent damage.

We reached the yard and found no one to support us. I ordered the cargo door open, and we were almost surprised by a military platoon that managed to penetrate the airport after armed resistance from the defence and to our luck: Babu and Germam Holt were armed to the teeth and started the defence of the Hercules.

Mark Kurt and I sprang into action with our Belgian rifles, firing and causing five casualties. Germam Holt, realising we could unload, released the cargo from the floor of the Hercules. Those interested in the goods turned up and in less than twenty minutes the cargo left the airport. There were many fuel leaks and we needed to refuel. Babu went to the fuel terminal and found that one of the tanker trucks was loaded. My faithful African friend pulled out the wires below the truck's flywheel axle and did the traditional hot-wiring. That African was a rare diamond!

The damage to the fuselage was remarkable. The steering rudder had four punctures, and under the right wing, there were numerous other punctures in the tanks and loss of fuel. Germam Holt ordered Babu to refuel Full Tanks, and so he did. His order was coherent, as we would lose fuel through the perforations during the return attempt. Due to being unladen, the Hercules was less heavy, plus the number three engine was in pieces and inoperative. Parasitic drag would cause high fuel consumption and limit flight level.

When Babu finished refuelling, he disconnected the hoses and closed the Hercules' fuel station. The tanker truck was far enough away from the aircraft when a medium calibre mortar hit it and blew it up, and next, we saw other mortars rushing into the yard.

Mark Kurt and I managed to start the engines while Germam Holt was preparing to close the main cargo door and waiting for Babu. At that moment I received word that my faithful African friend was down in the yard. I immediately relinquished command of the Hercules and ordered Mark Kurt to start taxiing to the headland and ran desperately through the cargo bay while the main cargo door was still open. I remember Germam Holt shouting at me to leave him behind, but I paid no attention to him and got out of the Hercules towards Babu. I lifted him with all my strength and carried him over my left shoulder as his blood dripped onto my shirt.

On my right came two Africans with their bloody AK-47s firing like two angry devils. I pulled out my inseparable forty-five calibre pistol and aimed, but it was Germam Holt, who, running and screaming, fired his Belgian automatic rifle ripping the arm off one of them and sifting the other from his right thigh to his chest.

The Hercules was moving under Mark Kurt's command. Our distance was nearly fifty metres from the main cargo door. Germam Holt guarded our rear and fired at seven Africans who mounted a heavy calibre machine gun. One of them prepared a Soviet RPG model rocket launcher and if it managed to hit the Hercules, we would be captured and then our end. Germam Holt was out of ammunition and shouted at me to get rid of the automatic rifle; he positioned himself on his knees with my rifle and aimed, after selecting for non-automatic firing. When I looked back I saw an African get hit by a shot to the head and at that moment, I realised we would get out of that hell alive by running towards Hercules.

Germam Holt commanded the main cargo door to go up and locked it. Their machine gun was firing at the Hercules non-stop. The German wielded one of the fifty-millimetre calibre side machine guns and wiped them out.

Babu was wounded below the left collarbone, in addition to other wounds: in his right thigh and transected on the side of his waist. He had lost a lot of blood. At first, I thought I had hit him in the Femoral vein, but luckily not. I quickly stopped the bleeding and loaded him on a stretcher with intravenous medication and saline solution. I got into the cockpit and took command of the Hercules. I was right about Mark Kurt. It was no accident that I had chosen him to fly with me on suicide missions to the core of hell, where African devils awaited us.

When I lined up with the axis of the runway, I accelerated two of the three engines to full throttle and completed the third while avoiding power asymmetry. The Hercules raced down the runway for take-off, but at the very moment I pulled the stick towards me a mortar passed in front of us to crash onto the runway and crater enough to prevent our take-off; yet the Hercules was flying and climbing with the maximum power available from all three engines, even though one of the landing gear had not collected. I ordered Mark Kurt to leave it where it was.

Our escape was not easy. The high-calibre anti-aircraft batteries resumed a brutal charge of fire hitting the Hercules from all sides. I said to Mark Kurt: "They want to bring us down at any cost, but that won't be today." Then the aircraft received an impact that made it shudder violently, and a fire broke out on board. Germam Holt, with the courage of the demigod Achilles, took on another challenge and on his return was covered in black soot, earning him the nickname: *Smoke*.

We reached the territory of Zaire keeping FL150 in an unpressurised flight. An hour and a half into the flight, we lost engine number four due to low lubricating oil pressure and were definitely in an emergency with two engines inoperative and one landing gear locked down, just another stroke of luck.

With thirty-five nautical miles to go to "Base of Operations", Mark Kurt tried a VHF contact and told Akin that we were in an emergency and with Babu injured, which required the preparation of a vehicle to take him to the Central Hospital in Kinshasa. My bet was exactly to land and survive.

After all the procedures I did a detailed briefing: in case of a crash everyone was to abandon the aircraft without looking back, and I would be in charge of Babu. I saw for the first time something that scares men: the fear of dying. The Hercules was limited to small, inclined turns due to the loss of symmetrical power but compensated enough to maintain a flight in line with the axis of the runway. There was a clear emotional strain and we were left to make the best of it. Germam Holt alerted us that the fuel was running out alarmingly, which led me to consider that more punctures were added to the ones that were already there as we took off and to be honest: we were almost out of fuel and there was no chance of a go-around for a new climb, approach and landing procedure.

Germam Holt kept all the fuel valves open and tried at all costs to balance the weight between the wings and avoiding tendencies. At that point, we wanted to land however, we could and survive. I ordered the landing gear down, which luckily came down and locked down.

At one thousand five hundred feet, the number two engine stopped running due to lack of fuel, and the asymmetry trend was noticed immediately. Nothing that couldn't be corrected with Rudder and an Ailerons compensator, as well as with power ahead with the one engine running to maintain final speed when crossing the landing headland. I let the Hercules touch down on the runway and decelerate to a definitive stop. At the end of the runway, I entered the intersection, continued through the yard and finally parked and applied the brakes without any further manoeuvres.

I turned off the only running engine. The fuel pump lamps

were on for low-pressure effect as there was no more fuel in the tanks. I went in search of my loyal African friend Babu and found him awake with a smile on his face despite his injuries, and we carefully carried him to the vehicle to be transferred to the Central Hospital in Kinshasa. When the pilots, flight engineers and mechanics saw the state of the Hercules, they could not believe it was possible to fly it in those conditions. There were no parts that were not damaged. It would take weeks of repairs and replacement of parts, such as the engine, which was totally destroyed. I gave orders to tow the Hercules to the hangar, and there the wounds would be treated and healed. Once again, like the Phoenix, the Hercules would rise from the ashes.

Under the gaze of all, I consecrated myself, and those who accompanied me were in the hall of the invincible and implacable aces, in which only one mercenary stands. Germam Holt, the German, would forever be Smoke. He was filled with pride at being part of the stories and adventures alongside a man called Captain and said he still had a lot to tell his grandchildren one day. I would make vows, but to do so it was imperative to get out of the African hell alive.

Chapter 7.

The B707 commanded by João Guedes was in Addis Ababa. There some technical difficulties arose to solve a malfunction that presented itself. The flight would carry radioactive cargo, which, as far as I knew, had initially departed from Baghdad, Iraq, and would continue to Pretoria, South Africa, but with a stopover at the "Base of Operations". The reason: the South African government had new requirements for receiving the radioactive cargo, and the negotiations were at a standstill; however, the Ethiopian government did not want that cargo on its territory. The claim did not convince me because we keep that kind of cargo close to us, mainly because of the international interests in radioactive cargo.

Take-off from Addis Ababa was normal and the flight proceeded as planned. During descent and approach for landing, Akin received a VHF contact from João Guedes. He reported that there was an intense fire on board and a lot of black smoke, although the mechanic Tatus was trying to fight the fire but had not returned from the cargo sector. João Guedes considered Tatus to be dead. His crew consisted of Co-pilot Igor Kracoviv and Flight Engineer Velasquez. I was alerted by Akin and made my way to our small communications tower and managed to talk to João Guedes. He was calm, although I knew his time had come.

Using binoculars, I could see the B707 with its tail on fire and dense black smoke. By my calculations, the elevator control cable and rudder were compromised and performances deteriorated. I could see the B707 approaching in a desperate turn when João Guedes said over the radio: "I am leaving this world today. Take care of my family, my friend. May God receive me in peace from this hell."

The B707 tilted beyond the maximum angle. There was a clear attempt to control it, but a violent yaw demonstrated an aircraft out of control, unsupported by the high pitch and at low altitude. Like a butcher's knife, the right wing ripped through the earth two miles from the headland, enveloped in a giant fireball, ending in a devastating and definitive explosion.

I felt the loss of all the crew members very deeply. Years later, I hired a renowned company to investigate the "accident": it was discovered that the B707 would never reach any destination, on orders from a very powerful intelligence agency.

João Guedes' wife received the news with great regret and I warned her that I would send an air ticket to Montevideo, Uruguay, as we needed to talk and deal with matters of interest to her and her son, Bruno. The other families received the same treatment as João Guedes' family. Tatus' family was illiterate and decided to provide their children with an education for the rest of their lives, and only when trained and educated would they receive what their father had earned through hard work and with his own life. Tatus' wife started receiving anonymously a reasonable sum to live on, but the money led her to drugs and death.

The Iranian immediately made another B707 available for flight operations and made no comment or mention of the dead. The redemption of the monies deposited in the British bank was another matter he did not care about. With what I had accumulated from salaries, I used some of it to buy out the bank manager and unlock the deposits in bank accounts for the families. For this, I used a law firm in London, which later became part of my business. I could use other more radical methods to unlock the money, but I needed to conduct everything in the "civilised western world" in a way that kept the focus on what was yet to be conquered.

I learned that I would be getting a replacement crew. Before it arrived I gathered my men and, after honouring the dead and friends, decided to communicate that other crew members would be arriving soon. The men were very cohesive and did not speak up. When I moved on to another subject the stars twinkled in each of their eyes and for the first time, I stated that I was working on a unique and definitive mission and that I was counting on each of them. That would be the passport to a new life far from that hell.

After two weeks Babu returned to the "Base of Operations" recovered. He received all the pampering he deserved. My faithful African friend had tears in his eyes upon seeing me. As I had never seen him crying, I jokingly stated to relax him: "I thought your tears were black too." He, simply, hugged me for the first time. I took it as a gesture of friendship and respect.

He said: "The Captain saved my life, the Captain has not abandoned me, the Captain is my brother in life and death, the Captain has my infinite loyalty."

The great conquerors of the past, though cruel, knew that the loyalty of the soldiers depended on winning every heart, not with words in the wind, but with acts of bravery and justice. I had a small army, which I called the *"Legion of Misfits"*, and ready to act under my leadership. Boma was the ultimate destination for our escape from African hell.

My plans did not include the new crew members; I would

occupy them with all sorts of activities justified by their being novices: seniority is rank and stony privilege. The flights to Europe were intended for them and away from the theatre of action that interested me and on some flights I included our cargo accompanied by a crewman who guaranteed payment and loading, as well as imposing on my men the silence of a dictator.

I needed an "operations strategist" and to this end, I designated Paul Levi to talk to me in the "Administration House". The Israeli met me and sat in one of the armchairs in front of my desk. I explained what I had in mind and waited for him to speak. Paul Levi was a man of action, intelligent and cautious. He, with all his characteristic calmness, stated that the plan was bold and there was a good chance of success and it was at this point that I tasked him to handle the strategy of action in detail and trim edges, but would only reveal the plan to the men a few hours before the start of actions in Boma.

Before my "operations strategist" left, I handed him Babu's report on Boma and ordered my faithful African friend to report to the "Administration House" and told him what Paul Levi's role would be. From that moment on Babu would assist him. In all we were twenty men, that is if we did not have more casualties until we put the intended mission into practice.

I knew that Paul Levi would ask me for the ground plan of the building in Boma, but when I read Babu's report I realised that it contained details of the utmost importance. In the front garden of the building was a metal plaque bearing the name of the architectural and engineering company, based in Antwerp, Belgium, which planned and built the building. The floor plan, side sections and structural engineering calculations were certainly not on file at the Kinshasa administration, but at the company's headquarters and the urban public administration of the city of Antwerp. To obtain a copy one would have to travel to that pleasant city, besides considering the possibility of some significant and secret construction modifications that might have taken place; which is not to say that no records existed.

The name of the firm responsible for the planning and construction was Clarryon & Broskley, which was housed in a modern building in the centre of the Belgian city. The commercial flight to Brussels was half an hour later than scheduled that Tuesday morning. My connection to Antwerp was by train and I stayed in a hotel that was comfortable enough, clean enough and close enough to the train station. My first foray was to the real estate file of the city hall and, as luck would have it, I was attended by a nice young lady. Her eyes were dark green, light brown hair with a Chanel-like cut; she wore light red lipstick and had perfectly manicured nails. Women like compliments on the beauty and personal care, this sin is called: "female vanity".

Despite being a public department, the place seemed to be of little demand, and this fact allowed me to talk about banal and unimportant matters with her. It was not difficult to find out her name, as it was on the work table: *Mlle. Desire*. She asked: "Well? What do you wish?" I was careful to explain simply that I needed to obtain a copy of the floor plan of a building to confer the design with the current construction and to deal with building insurance. Mlle. Desire kept her dark green eyes in my direction for a few "long" seconds while the fingers of her right hand moved in sequence over the service counter; her well-manicured fingernails were clipping, showing unparalleled skill.

She asked flatly: "Is that all you want from me?" I left Antwerp the next morning, but beforehand I paid the hotel bill and warned that the "miss" would sleep late. The hotel attendant let an almost childish smile draw on his effeminate-faced lips; I did not mind his inelegance, however, with me was the full floor plan of the building in Boma and more than I could have imagined. Mlle. Desire confessed that it was unusual for that request and should follow a bureaucratic process, but I compensated her with an envelope containing one thousand US dollars and a night of pleasures accompanied by two bottles of French champagne. They say: "Every man has his price." It is true! Even women!

I stayed in a hotel in the centre of Brussels and looked for the address of the company that manufactured the machinery I had brought from Tripoli. On boarding the machinery at the airport, I found a nameplate with the Part Number and Serial Number, the name of the manufacturing company and the address of the head office. My objective was to obtain an informative catalogue of that machinery, as it would confirm exactly that the high investment of the purchase by the mining company would be compensated in the obtaining of the final product, and much more than one can imagine.

I asked for a taxi at the hotel reception desk, which did not take long and got into the Peugeot. As soon as it moved in the direction of the main street I informed the driver of the address; it was not difficult to find the company situated on Rue Dukesnoy. I asked the driver to wait and he kindly nodded. I entered the medium-sized building. A spacious hall with a few low tables and chairs served as a place for customers to sit until they were served. On the small tables were magazines, folders and magazines from the world of mechatronics. To my total satisfaction, there was a very detailed catalogue with the respective Part Numbers as part of the advertisement. I didn't waste any time, and as it was exposed to the public, I understood that I could borrow it, and so I did.

Inside the moving taxi, I leafed through the company catalogue: Holman & Holman. And there was the photograph and the Part Number, which I compared with my notes. Turning the pages and found a detailed description of what it was for. There was no doubt about the reason for the purchase, as well as the secretive place it was destined for.

I returned to Kinshasa the next day on a commercial flight and brought with me the blueprint of a company called Belgique Minèire, whose building was constructed in Boma by the firm Clarryon & Broskley. The activity of the Belgique Minèire was the extraction and cutting and storage of diamond, which were the most valuable in the world, unequalled by the mines in South Africa, and with absolute secrecy to prevent anyone from discovering their unique origin, in the territory of Zaire. My suspicions and calculations were right and the story told by Babu was true.

I'm talking about the sum of seven hundred and fifty million US dollars in perfect diamond, the purest ever seen by human eyes. And who would pay that amount for diamonds? Well, before I sell them, I have to steal them! The business world works in mysterious ways, and to the layman everything is illogical.

There was no reason for excitement, but for planning and work. The building plans would be for Paul Levi as part of his operational requirements. He and Babu would travel south to Boma and make a study of the theatre of actions and as part of the information base, they would discuss with me the possible plan of action and escape.

One very important detail was the two-way tunnel that connected the building to the diamond mine, with a length of four hundred and thirty linear metres, a modern and efficient transport system and a platform in both directions, which allowed the movement of people. At a depth of one and a half metres, the platform had monorails where the material for extracting the diamond was moved. For me, it was not the extraction that mattered, but the depositing of the diamonds ready for sale.

The owners of Belgique Minèire did not save money to make a quick profit from the extraction, as the whole process was down to automation and purity checks and the proposed cutting project to get the most out of the "shiny little stones".

The main plan showed the extension of the building on the land, well-guarded by security guards of a private company also Belgian, whose name was: Sécurité des Biens. And believe me, the insurer of the Belgique Minèire was Sécurité des Biens. It was exactly one of the cross-section plans that definitively showed that part of the building was missing. How is that possible? Let me explain: Mlle. Desire, when accessing the plans, noticed that there was an additional and separate file inside a folder with the print "Confidentiel Sécurité". And let's just say that, by some chance, and after once again she had cum naked on me on the bed in the hotel room, she confessed that she had included a file because she considered it "very important" for me. She was right: I love intelligent women!

By superimposing the additional floor plan over the side plan, one could see an intermediate floor: in the shape of a parallelepiped; it was a safe large enough for a man to stand on. The additional floor plan was folded in such a way that when you opened it you could see the safe from the front. And the most interesting thing was that the name of the maker of the chest was recorded: Fabergé. I believe in allusion to the "Fabergé Eggs".

Chapter 8.

In Cape Town, there lives to this day my gunsmith, now quite old, besides his youngest son, who has followed his father's profession. They live a comfortable life. Two days after arriving in Kinshasa I travelled to Cape Town and went to visit my gunsmith friend. His welcome was always warm and an enviable smile with his teeth like ivory. I took advantage of the trip to bring some gifts for his children, there were nine in total. He knew that visit had another purpose, for he did not see my gun, and would only take it to him in case of an irreparable defect by me.

The South African asked: "What is the reason for your visit?"

I replied: "Business."

And with a gentle gesture with his right arm, he indicated the wide veranda with two comfortable chairs for us to talk, accompanied by a small table with a teapot with tea, cups, small spoons, sugar cubes and cornflour biscuits made by his wife. I certainly wasn't interested in "five o'clock tea".

I told him that I needed a man capable of opening a Fabergé safe and that I was willing to pay him well, including him as a middleman, if everything went well. The gunsmith remained thoughtful, looking far away, and sometimes drank his tea, served by his wife. He unabashedly said: "Captain, we have known each other for many years and know how much I can trust you. I know who can do this job, however, the price is high."

Next, I stated: "Money is no problem."

To my surprise, the gunsmith called out his name: Mpumelele. Like lightning, the boy was in front of his father. He was his eldest son. Mpumelele's credentials were presented, and I was impressed; however, I once again made sure to warn that this was a Fabergé safe. The gunsmith allowed his son to speak and explained the whole mechanism of closing, locking, locking and unlocking that safe and finally said: "There are only four safes of this model at present. The safe with end two, I unlocked it for a company in Pretoria, due to a mistake by the white official."

At that moment I had a concern to resolve. They knew Mpumelele, and if the matter came to light after the theft, because it was a Fabergé safe, he could be arrested and interrogated. Certainly, I would be denounced.

I asked the gunsmith about it. He told me something that only a very lucky person could hear. I was a very lucky man indeed.

Mpumelele was a triplet of univitelline formation, that is, the three children were the same. So what? The gunsmith told me that one of the triplet brothers did not live in Cape Town and the neighbours did not know about the triplets because, to them, the gunsmith's family had twin sons and the other seven sons with the second wife, totalling nine children; but the gunsmith had ten children. I concluded that at the time of the action Mpumelele's brother would take his place; neighbours could attest to the presence of "Mpumelele". Why did one of the brothers not live in Cape Town? Simple: that brother preferred to live with his mother, who was the gunsmith's first wife.

The gunsmith's thoughtful attitude before answering was

exactly because he had considered the possibility of that "manoeuvre" at that moment; and I understood his reason for saying that the amount charged was high, as it would be multiplied four times due to the inclusion of the three brothers and the "breeder's fees". Fair, very fair!

I agreed with the gunsmith. He did not ask me how much I would pay for the service; not that he did not want to know. To end the conversation, I offered the payment of five hundred thousand US dollars. We sealed our agreement with a handshake, but first I said: "If you betray me, I will come after you, and you will see what I am capable of."

The gunsmith replied: "I have no doubts, nor does my son."

As part of the agreement, I would send a telegram in advance, in which I advised when the "safe-cracker" should be ready, and the other brother would join the gunsmith. I know there was a great risk, as I have always considered that there is no perfect and infallible plan, however, there was a good chance that it would go well, especially for the amount agreed upon. What I did not reveal to the gunsmith was where the action would be; I would arrange for Mpumelele to travel to Zaire to join me, and it would certainly not be on a first-class commercial flight, but on one of our flights back from South Africa, as a stowaway and with no record of entry into Zaire. For me, that would not be a problem.

I always took care of my company in Cape Town through my Jewish accountant, who gave "financial life" to the company with inflows and outflows of money and sometimes even took part in public tenders and private business deals with the company in the field of exports and imports, as well as passing on the payment of taxes to the government. My objective was to continue as a "safe harbour" for the capital inflow that I accumulated with my share in the business arising from our cargo and to keep up with the monthly payments to Dom Antonino in Sicily. As I said, it is respect for these powerful people that keeps the business going, as I am not comfortable with a price on my head, especially when it comes to the Sicilian Mafia.

You might even take a chance on getting the wife of one of them into bed. No doubt that they will know: a woman always tells on her tongue, and the "soldiers", those of the "lower clergy", will know because he who has a mouth speaks! As long as it is not the betrayed husband who knows, you will be seen as lucky; but if you betray a boss or fail to pay his share in the business; then consider yourself a dead man and about to "eat grass by the root"; that is if they bury you decently.

I once again returned to Zaire. On arrival at the "Base of Operations", the B707 was taking off bound for Belgrade and the DC8 refuelling for take-off bound for Kiev, USSR, now the capital of Ukraine. The crews of both aircraft were made up of "rookie" crew members, and so we kept them away from my plans for Boma, while one of my men followed the mission.

During the return to the "Base of Operations" I considered the possibility of using two helicopters, but only had one. I knew that between the village of Lóvua and Chitato, Angola, to the North and near the Zaire border, there was an Angolan military base with three well-armed Soviet Mig-8 model helicopters, with enough capacity to transport part of my men. My objective was to steal a Mig-8 and hide it until the day of the mission in Boma, and for that, I needed a pilot. Two men were helicopter pilots and I did not know if either of them flew the Soviet models. I ordered Babu to call Kauffman and Kruger to report to the "Administration House".

The two Germans presented themselves in front of my desk,

and I ordered them to sit in the armchairs; under Babu's gaze I got straight to the point and asked, "Which of the two is capable of flying a Soviet Mig-8 model helicopter?" Kauffman immediately qualified.

Having no other option, I accepted his madness, but Kruger, with his suspicious look and agile thought, asked: "Shall we borrow it from our neighbour?"

He was referring to Angola since it is militarily supplied by Cubans and Soviets. I looked at Kruger and gave him enough of a smile to understand that the answer was: "Yes." Kauffman got a startled look on his face and mouth ajar as if he couldn't believe it. My gaze went inside Kauffman's soul: "Did you think you would do a course in the USSR? No, you won't. We're going to steal a Mig-8." I have never seen Kruger laugh so hard at his brother, and after they withdrew it was Babu's turn to imitate the German's face.

My faithful African friend Babu brought a map so we could get the approximate distance from the "Base of Operations" to a mid-point in northern Angola between the two villages and thus coordinate the action, which should be fast and efficient. I considered that the mission would be at night to avoid long combat, but I could not foresee the consequences of the helicopter theft. There was no doubt that the possibility of facing regular Cuban troops was a great challenge, if possible we should avoid them.

In Africa, at that time, the best infantry that existed was the Cuban, because they were brave, organised, cultured, well-led and prepared, in addition to the ideological encouragement based on the so-called "proletarian internationalism"; that is to say, the Cubans were driven by ideals, something that a mercenary abhors.

The work "*The Art of War*" demands that: "A general must know the enemy and if the enemy has superior potential one must avoid him until he can overcome him." I had no time to debate the military treatise written in the fourth century BC, by the Chinese strategist Sun Tzu. Nevertheless, I will opine: Sun Tzu was wrong in that sense, for I needed a Soviet helicopter to make up my battle group in Boma, not against Cuban infantry.

That night I met with Paul Levi and ordered him to prepare a raid on the Angolan military base and do all the surveying to plan the theft of the helicopter. He and Babu would use one of the vehicles for transport, armaments, supplies, fuel and water. Both of them stayed for four consecutive days observing the movement of the Angolan military base, and on the fifth day, they returned. Their account motivated me to pursue the theft of the helicopter, because in the four days that the base was observed, only on one day did one of the helicopters take off for a short flight, indicating little fuel supply, little interest in armed conflict and a lack of leadership routine. The pilots were Angolans between the ages of twenty-five and thirty, with a garrison of fifteen men as crew, three mechanics and a military officer at the rank of Lieutenant.

The first concern would be with the fuel on board the helicopter to be stolen, as shortages could compromise the mission. I'm referring to a crash by dry run. I decided that one of the vehicles would be prepared with two hundred-litre barrels of aviation paraffin at a point before the border and in Zairean territory. Something that could not be avoided was the noise of the engines during departure. My men would only fire if it was necessary to intimidate the Angolans or defend ourselves. I had not gone soft: the objective was the theft of the Soviet helicopter, as there was no reason to kill them; but if they insisted on being heroes: "I would open the gates of hell for each one of them."

I chose a place to refuel in case it was necessary, and in that place Akin would remain with the vehicle and the two barrels containing fuel. On noticing the approach of the stolen helicopter, he would light four points with fire demarcating a square to affect the landing. We set off in the early evening with the two vehicles: Akin was at the wheel of one of the vehicles accompanied by Paul Levi, and Babu was at the wheel of the other with Kauffman, Kruger and me. When we arrived at the chosen point, we helped Akin prepare the site and when everything was ready we set off.

We crossed the border and left our vehicle off the road ready to go, while Paul Levi led us through the terrain. Everyone was very well armed and determined. After climbing an elevation of approximately seventy metres, we reached the top and between the trees, we could see the Angolan military base due to the lighting: a wooden house that served as a dormitory, canteen and administration and a mobile tank that indicated it was destined for the helicopters' fuel, there was no hangar and no Angolan man standing guard at night. It was a serious breach of their security.

I ordered Babu to remain on the summit and that when he saw us take off, he should return to the "Base of Operations" with the vehicle. My faithful African friend did not like this, since he was passionate about helicopters. The disappointment was stamped on his face. I looked into his eyes and said: "Babu, go back to Base of Operations with the vehicle. That is an order! But I promise you that you will be in the cockpit of the mission to come." My faithful African friend cracked a childish smile, showing his ivory-coloured teeth, and accepted the order.

We descended the lift with all due care and ready to strike

back at any attack. The three helicopters were positioned side-by-side. For security reasons, we chose the one that was furthest away from the Angolan military's house. It was not difficult to loosen the ropes that tied them to the ground. The access door was locked, but with a crowbar, we easily forced it open. Paul Levi got into the helicopter to pull out the contact wires for departure. Kauffman followed him, while Kruger and I were in a defensive position with our right knees resting on the ground with our Belgian rifles unlocked and pointed at the Angolan military's home. Paul Levi managed to close the electrical contact and said to Kauffman: "Now it's up to you."

This was a very curious scene: Kauffman was the son of an ex-Nazi and Paul Levi the son of a Jewish survivor of one of the Nazi concentration camps.

Kauffman was cultured. In addition to his native language, he mastered other languages, including Russian. He commanded the battery switch to ON and from one moment to the next I heard in the silence of the night the gears of the main rotor moving, as well as those of the tail rotor. The noise began to increase and was gaining speed of rotation. The lights of the Angolan military house were switched on, and the inevitable was about to happen.

The main rotor was quickly stabilised and ready to go. Out of the house came a few armed Angolans in their underwear. Kruger and I started firing in automatic sequence to scare them off, but it seems they were willing to be heroes: fighting back with everything they had. We wasted no time and loaded our Belgian rifles with grenades and threw them simultaneously, to create an intimidating effect, and set off inside the Mig-8 while Paul Levi gave us cover.

We entered the Soviet helicopter, which was now beginning to climb and gaining altitude. I saw one of the Angolan pilots pointing an RPG rocket launcher. So, I selected for a shot to shot firing and aimed with my Belgian rifle, with the helicopter moving. The aiming strap crossed exactly the unfortunate man's head, there was no alternative: I pressed down with all determination, and the projectile hit him as I set out. The Angolan's head was thrown back, yet he managed to shoot and almost hit us as he passed over the helicopter cockpit.

Kauffman was definitely in control of the Mig-8, accelerating it to leave the combat perimeter; and as we passed over the elevation I saw Babu running towards the vehicle in the direction of the border. At that moment I heard our German pilot shout: "We are almost out of fuel, I don't know if we will reach the support point." Kruger spoke harshly in German to his brother. And silence took over the Mig-8.

We were flying at low altitude and high speed; after a few minutes, we crossed the border and spotted the square with the four fire points. The low fuel pressure lamp was flashing on the panel, but Kauffman was willing to show the skill of a good pilot and made the landing on the square when the rotors stopped working. My other faithful African friend brought the car around and prepared to refuel with help from Paul Levi.

Something flashed through my mind like a meteor: the Angolan pilots knew that the helicopter was low on fuel and that we would have to land soon after the escape take-off. Nothing was stopping them from coming after us. I ordered them to hold a defensive position while they refuelled. Kruger brought an RPG rocket launcher with four projectiles that were inside the helicopter. In few minutes after landing the second barrel of paraffin started to be pumped into the Mig-8's fuel tank; then I heard the noise of two enemy Mig-8s looking for us.

They detected us easily and positioned themselves to start

the attack in flight. The first burst of fire came from the gunner's machine gun, but with terrible aim. Kruger with the loaded rocket launcher fired mercilessly. What I saw was a demolishing impact followed by an explosion that ripped off the tail and rear rotor of the enemy helicopter, crashing violently against the ground, killing all on board.

The other helicopter started a manoeuvre aimed at preventing our escape. We fired our rifles at that war machine while Akin bravely continued the supply, but the African received two shots in the back. Luckily, it did not hit the fuel tank, while Paul Levi was firing relentlessly in a counter-attack.

Kruger received a shot in the right shoulder and another in the left forearm as he tried to reposition the shell in the rocket launcher. Kauffman rushed out of the cockpit to rescue him while my body lay over Akin's to protect him. The sadistic gunner was firing to annihilate us when a pair of speeding lights stopped a few metres from me and Akin. A military boot touched the dirt floor, and an African with an RPG on his shoulder made a spectacular shot towards the enemy Mig-8, hitting the cockpit, followed by a big explosion that lit up what was left of the night on the African savannah. It was Babu, my faithful African friend, saving our lives.

Paul Levi took over the refuelling vehicle and set off towards Base of Operations", as did Babu in the other vehicle. Kauffman managed to start up the Mig-8 and on board were the two wounded: Akin and Kruger. I remained beside my wounded men. I ordered Kauffman to move at high speed to the "Base of Operations", as we did not have the autonomy to fly straight ahead from Kinshasa, and unfortunately, there was no one in the communications tower. But I knew that the Bell UH-1 helicopter was fuelled and had the range to Kinshasa.

Kauffman landed the Mig-8 at the "Base of Operations" near the Bell, and we transferred the wounded. In less than ten minutes we were flying with a bow to Kinshasa. We landed in the car park of the Central Hospital and were assisted by nurses and doctors. Akin had lost a lot of blood, as had Kruger. Bell's floor was witness to the plight of both.

Paul Levi stayed at the "Base of Operations" and with express orders to hide the Mig-8 helicopter. I later learned that some Soviet Mig-21 fighter planes coming from Angola flew over Zaire territory looking for the stolen Mig-8. Our madness could have serious consequences, but we would have to wait and give time to time. The presence of my wounded men would draw attention and alert the Zairean authorities. To neutralise any future onslaught, there were two circumstances to consider: first, when we arrived at the hospital everyone would know we were mercenaries, and with this fear was useful. The second, some authority would demand a "shut my mouth" compensation, and it didn't take long for one of these "smart guys" to appear. What I do know is that the last time I saw him he was hanging by his ankles and without his head. That's what I always say: "There are people who lose their heads over little things."

It was time to let the dust settle and my wounded men recover. They spent a few weeks on "holiday" in hospital, with care and pampering from the nurses. Have no doubt that everyone on the medical staff received their respective and well deserved "bonuses". Akin was operated on twice and recovered, as did Kruger. During this period "we behaved", although that incursion into Angola made me lose precious time, because I had to wait for the recovery of the wounded, but as they say: "Everything has its time." The time was ripe to effectively organise the mission in Boma: "To take one step back, to take two or more ahead."

My gunsmith was certainly worried, so to avoid unnecessary worries I sent him a telegram. The Mig-8 remained stowed among some trees under a military mesh as camouflage, so as not to be detected. Kauffman's behaviour was extraordinary and he came to have my regard at Kruger's level, and this would yield a special friendship in the future. And what about Babu? All of us who were present in that action, and alive to this day, know how much we owe him: simply life.

The Iranian was pleased with the flight operations and how it turned into profits. The B707 and DC8 flew almost daily, and the load distribution was close to the maximum load, so much so that he asked me about the possibility of another DC8. When he asked my opinion, I answer to wait another six months. The Iranian remained silent while I waited to hear from him. The answer was a simple "All right", and we said goodbye.

The conversation with the Iranian was technical and commercial, but at no time did he comment on the recent events in Kinshasa. I'm not so naïve as to believe that he did not have informers everywhere. The landing of our helicopter in the car park of the Central Hospital in Kinshasa was reported by Tousset, that was true, but if there is one thing I have always abhorred in a man, it is to be a snitch. Why did the Iranian make no comment to me? He was receiving information from Tousset and if he commented on what had happened he would put the life of his "soft-spoken employee" in danger because he knew what I was capable of doing.

Tousset was useful and would be instructed to know what exactly happened, however, I was the guarantee of increasing profits and the demand was increasing for the just-in-time deliveries services, which not even Fedex has. The Iranian preferred to keep the suppliers and customers happy through his "business manager" in Africa and see his bank account receive the profits, still, no one is irreplaceable, and I had never been more motivated to continue my plan for Boma.

I decided to gather all the crew and mechanics on a hot summer Saturday for a lunch with lots of beef, gaucho barbecue style, and beer. Akin was recovered from his injuries. He was happy to take care of every detail and at that meeting, I told the crew that there was a long flight schedule and we would follow it to the best of our ability. Not every crew member would be part of my battlegroup in Boma and my men knew that silence was not optional. The interaction was inevitable, just as betrayal is the sister of loyalty: always at odds with each other.

Don't forget that the greatest betrayals in human history have occurred within families; people of the same blood. Why not have a Judas among us? There is a very simple detail: I have never been willing to be crucified!

There are two types of men: those who are prey and those who are predators. In this case, I preferred to be a predator, and I was careful to avoid a role reversal, and as my paternal grandfather used to say: "We are remembered for our mistakes." Wrong. Nobody remembers a loser. In my case, the mistake would lead to death. In Africa in those days there was no time for philosophising; only determination would make you a survivor.

Flights to Eastern Europe, USSR, and North African Arab countries filled the aircraft holds with our cargo. My profits deposited in South Africa reached a figure of three hundred and thirty-two million US dollars. My Jewish accountant arranged for the opening of an offshore company in the Bahamas and transferred half the amount to a bank account in that nice island in the Caribbean Sea, where secrecy was one of the most legitimate and upright principles of the capitalist status I now enjoyed.

In Uruguay, where the laws of the tax haven also reign: thirty million US dollars of my total capital was received without questions and I started speculating in the economy of countries like Brazil, where it is legitimate to plunder the people and get rich: "men of the financial market". I remember that was what they called us when the truth of the facts meant: to be of the "financial elite of speculation". The options were many: buying and selling dollars, oil, gas, oil platforms, aviation, commodities, communication technology, construction, among many others. That country has Africa in its blood, the characterless avarice of the European conqueror, subservience to capital and incalculable natural wealth.

I looked at Brazil as a continental country to be raped as many times as its own people would allow. It was the perfect breeding ground for the corrupt and the corruptors. Remember, my only intention was to "invest", that's all. At what cost to them? Simple: whatever they were willing to pay. Now my capital was playing the role of a bank; "selling money", and for that, there was a legion willing to buy it. I confess I never made so much money without having to go after it. And the best way was always anonymity, because "what one hand does, the other doesn't need to know".

On one of the many warm African nights, Paul Levi came to me to request authorisation for another incursion into Boma, accompanied by Babu, and with the objective of a new land survey. I considered it important due to the time that had elapsed and authorised the incursion. They both left in two days and returned in five days with surprising information: a team of almost one hundred men were building an airstrip for executive jets; the work was well advanced and, according to Paul Levi's calculations, the airstrip would be ready in three months. The mining company was concerned about the safety of transporting rare and valuable diamonds.

Babu came to see me half an hour later and told me with concern that he had noticed an increase in the number of armed security men, in addition to the men working on the runway. What was the reason? My faithful African friend calculated approximately eighty men in total, shift relays every six hours as part of the routine and motorised surveillance around and no dogs. I considered the possibility that the extraction and obtaining of final polish had increased and would certainly also have increased the value in the gemstone market dominated by the Netherlands, Belgium, Israel and the USA, under the insoluble dominance of the Jewish origin families of the trade-in: gold, platinum and silver. To increase production one of the signs could be high demand, the stock of a durable good or the order of "investors". Who would this investor be? In case there was such an investor.

Before Babu left the "Administration House", I asked my faithful African friend if Paul Levi showed concern about the increased security manpower at the mining company. Babu looked at me and said: "No, not at any time; this is why I came to you and told Captain."

A paradox arose, which I would not put aside: I'm to this day very observant and cautious. Paul Levi brought me the action plan of the mission in Boma the next morning and after breakfast. The ex-Mossad prepared a sketch of the sector with details of the region, such as elevations, rivers, plains, bridges, roads, the proposed landing site and the entire mining complex, as well as the sectors under surveillance, terrain observation towers, entrance, number of vehicles and the number of security men, which was less than that stated by Babu. The Israeli explained the plan of action with aplomb and defined the attack structure

162

with two helicopters, complete personal armament, one thirty-millimetre calibre machine gun for each helicopter gunner, thirty-five Soviet RPG rocket launchers and high detonation power explosives.

He recommended the model of assault operations in the form of commandos, with the landing of the two helicopters inside the perimeter of the mining company, however, the approach for landing should occur with the demonstration of force, since it was impossible to avoid the noise of the helicopters' engines and rotors during the landing. For this, night or dawn action was the most advisable. The operation required a fast and efficient landing with displacement in two combat groups with the mission to eliminate any defence and attack with Soviet RPG, British-made Miller grenades and high fragmentation. The strategy was to terrorise the enemy, and if they resisted there would be no survivors.

The other group would maintain a perimeter of attack and defence and would not enter the building, this would have the largest number of men, heavily armed. The helicopter pilots would remain in their respective cockpit positions and take off after the landing. Paul Levi determined that the ground watch towers should be destroyed regardless of the type of resistance offered; the justification was to facilitate escape. The weaponry to be used was the Soviet RPG, capable of stopping a tank and shooting down an aircraft.

I followed the ex-Mossad's explanation attentively and watched him cautiously. The Israeli warned that after the first crucial minutes of combat enemy reinforcements could intensify, with the possibility of casualties. In this sense, he suggested intensive training and several simulations with some possible scenarios to evaluate the capacity to respond and resist the confrontation. Paul Levi made a decisive observation regarding the construction of the airstrip, due to the presence of many workers and other people who worked on the site without links to the mining company and armed security, and who could be victims of a brutal confrontation. In his view, we should wait until the work is finished.

It was a significant observation of great value and would avoid a massacre. I decided to postpone the action in Boma for "humanitarian reasons", nevertheless, I intensified the operations of nostra cargo, and maintain my monthly capitalisation, which yielded as much as that of a cocaine Baron in one of the Latin American countries, in addition to demanding from Paul Levi continuous training of "my men".

My off-shore company in the Bahamas, whose name was Enigma Enterprise Ltd, participated in the purchase of shares in promising companies in various sectors. My tentacles were expanding, and no one suspected, not even close, that a simple mercenary pilot was intervening in various sectors of various emerging country economies, even extracting whatever was convenient for me and with total obedience to the law. The financial power of the Enigma Enterprise was such that it acquired more than fifty per cent of the shares of certain companies; and with this came the power to decide their fate.

No one imagined that it was arms trafficking that made my company an enigma. In Europe, my tentacles ran deep while I lived on the African savannah as a simple "business manager" for the Iranian. I do not deny that he became a billionaire because the volume of war cargo he moved was greater than mine, but it was not a competition but a medium and long-term investment. It was at this time that I made one of the most important business decisions in Europe, with promising profitability and highly lucrative prospects. It was all a question of time to reap the results and achieve my goals.

Chapter 9.

I travelled to Brussels on business, where I stayed for a few days and then went on to London. There I bought a flat in the luxurious Chelsea neighbourhood in total anonymity, as well as an office in The City neighbourhood, close to business opportunities.

The Enigma Enterprise was present in the financial life of several important cities such as New York, Amsterdam, Brussels, Paris, São Paulo, Buenos Aires, Montreal, among others. Once I had another excellent opportunity to speculate in the emerging market of Brazil, from a brokerage house in New York. I speculated in the financial market by investing significant amounts in US dollars, the results were extraordinary and for the first time, I set aside a basic principle of the Zurich Axioms and risked more than ten per cent of net profit, breaking a "law" that I had always respected. The results were magnificent. With a simple command, all my speculative capital was back in my bank account, as was the net profit figure. Have no doubt that the New York brokerage firm as well as the affiliate were well rewarded. Remember: "For someone to win, someone has to lose."

Luck combined with speculative knowledge and intuition is like a Picasso painting: "Hard to understand, but when there is balance the result is as expected."

Of the "speculative investments" I found promising, and with an indication of certain profit, the telecommunications sector, which went hand in hand with the advance of technology.

When the mobile phone companies emerged, I had no doubts about wanting to be part of that world. In the vision of some, the future would be in the palm of my hand and with data traffic never seen by humanity. I was right.

My first contact with the high clergy of the Holy See was to deal with business. What was the business? Several, however, the one that caught my attention the most was real estate. I met Monsignor Lombardini, a man of faith, but in business, there is no room for that question so delicate to men: "Religion, politics and business don't mix." Wrong! Religion is one of the most profitable businesses in the world. Faith does not need to be financed, yet those who put themselves at the head of their "flocks" extort the followers without any scruples; of course, not all of them. This promiscuous extortion is as offensive and harmful as arms trafficking.

The difference between these gentlemen "anointed" in faith and an arms dealer is very interesting: "They sell faith in the name of life, and the dealer sells weapons in the name of death." It is as I heard from my friend Don Antonino: "They are just business." I agree!

Monsignor Lombardini confessed to me, and not that I'm a priest or have any vocational aptitude for the clergy, that there were serious financial difficulties in the Holy See. Direct financing would avoid going to the traditional banks, which, although it's a sin to charge interest, according to Pope Innocent III, are eager to sell money and charge interest, including to the Holy See. The contribution of a financial agent to cover deficits is dangerous for the borrower, but what is calculated in business is the risk of the lender, not the risk of the borrower. Our conversation took place on a walk in the garden. After the exposure of the "financial urgency", he, withdrew from the pocket of his elegant clerical gown a packet of cigarettes and when he tried to light a cigarette, I held his hand and said: "It is not good manners to smoke a cigarette in front of a guest. It's nothing persona." He used his common sense and put away the "Devil's Soother" back in the pocket of his clergy coat.

The amount is given by Monsignor Lombardini in the name of the Holy See as a loan request was a few million US dollars. My counterpart was the guarantees that I offered in the participation in the real estate sector. Monsignor Lombardini's eyes opened unexpectedly, showing a certain amazement, while I cynically awaited the answer of the "begging priest". The "yes" came next, as comes the day after the night, but in such delicate matters, what matters are signed papers, and this is what the lawyers of a powerful firm are for, who knows how to put every comma in its proper place, as well as the due percentage to collect and guarantee payment. I believe that the tithes and the Mass offerings do the rest and thus comply with a commercial agreement. It's not the crumbs that matter, it's the potential real estate.

That was the first of many loans. Besides Don Antonino in beautiful Sicily. He was pleased with his share of the profits. I knew exactly my place and, as I said, truth and respect make you the right man in business; this without directly involving the Cosa Nostra. A few years ago, my share in the real estate sector of the Holy See was thirty-eight per cent. Today the percentage is much higher because it's just business.

I took advantage of my stay in London to look up a long-time acquaintance. I won't reveal his name, since he is still the one who takes care of any document I urgently need, especially passports with another name and of the country I'm interested in.

Perfection is a matter of honour for him. The services he

provides are not for just anyone. I have never discussed the price, as it is worth every penny. Some intelligence agencies use his services to deal with these illegal matters and when a mission is classified as "unauthorised".

Many agents enter a country as "tourists" or as "students" with these passports, which are not registered by the government agency that controls the emissions, that is, fakes. No technology can stop an experienced forger, even with all the protections vaunted by political authorities, giving the feeling of "security". The counterfeiter uses advanced technology too and I do not recommend that you use illicit means to achieve any goals: "Do as I say, but do not do as I do."

Back to the African savannah. The Hercules was flying intensely and there was no shortage of tense and very dangerous moments. When I was away from the activity in Zaire it was because I was taking care of my business related with Enigma Enterprise and I left with Kruger the responsibility of the operations and negotiations.

My men were working hard and waiting to get out of that hell. Babu came to me, in the company of Paul Levi, to suggest a third visit to Boma to find out how the construction of the airstrip was going since almost three months had passed. I authorised it and asked them to pay attention to the safety level of the mining company. They left the next day and stayed for five days observing and taking notes of the site's routine.

During the period that Babu and Paul Levi were away, I took part in three delivery flights of our cargo. It honestly did not make sense to get involved in these dangerous missions, to the point of risking everything I was building, but in my blood ran the adventure and desire to fly, besides the importance for me of the respect of my men. My presence on those missions encouraged them and put me in the same level of danger. The damage to which the Hercules were subjected was visible, as well as the violence they used in an attempt to bring them down.

I was scheduled to fly to the western border of Uganda, with a scheduled landing near the town of Arua on a dirt airstrip eight hundred metres long. The cargo bay of the Hercules was at full capacity, in addition to our cargo, which was to be delivered North of the town of Ruhengeri, Rwanda. My crew consisted of Commander Mark Kurt, Flight Engineer Germam Holt and Master Loader and mechanic Mabetu.

We were aligned with the runway axis of the "Base of Operations" and ready for take-off. After the check-list, I throttled up the four powerful engines and we started the take-off run until we lifted the nose of the Hercules and climbed with a climb ratio of four hundred feet per minute, due to the take-off weight. Our watches indicated 05:10 a.m., and still, the African savannah was sleeping.

Sunrise in an aircraft cockpit is always a unique image, none is the same as the other day. After two hours we were close to the western border of Uganda and began the descent penetrating Ugandan airspace at ten thousand feet, cautiously continuing the descent until we reached three thousand feet and sighted the city of Arua. We stayed in the northern sector, making the traditional spiral descent with enough separation to line up at a short final landing position, with the landing gear lowered and locked in.

When crossing two thousand feet, in a curve, we received an impact on the left side of the Hercules that made it shake brutally. Gusts of anti-aircraft shells that crossed in front of us pierced the left side of the aircraft mercilessly. Without losing my cool I pushed the stick forward increasing the rate of descent looking for the first meters of the runway. Then another projectile hit the right side near the main cargo door, but a few meters from the ground I crossed the headland and forced the Hercules to execute an assault landing and immediately reverse, raising a curtain of red dust over the whole aircraft until almost the end of the runway. I executed a back-track and lined her up for take-off, as there was a tree on the headland opposite the landing, which would have prevented take-off due to its height. Hercules had the parking brake applied and the engines running.

Mabetu and Germam Holt opened the main cargo door and released the cargo latches to unload the cargo, while Mark Kurt and I took up position with our Belgian rifles, ready to defend the Hercules when a crowd of Africans in military uniforms appeared from the thicket and we narrowly missed some casualties. That was the gang that was coming to receive the package.

No matter the country, the boxes of weapons and ammunition disappeared within minutes of deliveries. As we closed the main cargo door we noticed the damage to the fuselage due to the projectiles. The impact on the right side meant that a pressurised flight was impossible, limiting us to fly below fifteen thousand feet; the fuel consumption would increase and the possibility of being detected and shot down. The only way out was to take off and maintain a westerly heading until we left Ugandan airspace and when in Zaire airspace turn southbound until we reached Lake Edward and, after crossing the lake in the same direction to its source, turn south-easterly and enter Rwandan airspace definitively with Ruhengeri heading.

We quickly took our seats in the cockpit and put on our seatbelts. We were ready to take off, however, in the direction of the sector from which the shots came during the final approach for landing. At the end of the runway a Soviet T-34 tank left over from World War II emerged from the woods, there was no room for questions and plans: I accelerated the Hercules' engines with full take-off power and we ran down the dirt runway, while the Soviet tank manoeuvred to line up and when it saw us it began to turn the turret of the seventy-six-millimetre cannon to fire.

The distance diminished by every second when, almost at the same time, I pulled the stick towards me with determination and causing the Hercules to raise its nose. A shot was fired from the T-34, which, I believe, must have passed within inches of the landing gear, or the intrassed of the aircraft's fuselage. Luck was once again on my side, however, what followed was the attempt to bring us down at any cost. Projectiles from the anti-aircraft batteries hit us across the length of the fuselage, as did all manner of shots. Five hundred feet above the ground, and with the landing gear already retracted, I began a left turn with maximum inclination and the engines at full throttle; the projectiles were climbing in search of us, however, on crossing one thousand five hundred feet with a west bow we were no longer targets for the ground troops and continued to climb to fifteen thousand feet and stabilise the Hercules precariously.

Germam Holt was wounded: one of the shells pierced the cockpit, and pieces of metal hit him in the left arm and chest. Part of the control panel of the pneumatic system was destroyed. Mabetu helped him, stopping the bleeding. I ordered Mark Kurt to pilot while I gave medical assistance to Germam Holt. It was also necessary to remove him from the cockpit, as the German, stubborn and proud, did not want to leave his position. I managed to stop the blood; the injuries were not deep, but he was hit in several places on his left arm and chest. The first aid kit was well supplied, which had been a requirement of mine from the beginning of the missions. Within minutes Germam Holt was properly attended to and I demanded that he rest while we took care of the flight.

Before leaving the cargo section where Germam Holt was, I looked at our cargo and assessed whether it was worth risking their lives in the state the Hercules was in and with a crew member injured. My conclusion was the same as always: "If you're in the rain, you're in it to get wet." Germam Holt would not forgive himself if I aborted the mission because of him. I knew him too well. He was one of my men who deserved to leave the African hell.

I returned to the cockpit while Mark Kurt piloted the Hercules on his arm, that is, the autopilot was inoperative. On entering Zaire airspace, he commanded a left turn to capture the southern bow, while I took over the Hercules' systems control panel from Germam Holt. I noticed that there was a small hydraulic leak and the fuel quantity indicators on the tanks were balanced, which indicated that despite the firing that the Hercules had been subjected to, there was no loss of fuel.

As we sighted Lake Edward to the east we were sure that we were in Zaire airspace. During the crossing, the B737-200 Adv crew made contact on VHF frequency 123.45. The Commander Jean-Pierre with his brother, Jean-Batiste, and Loader Master and -Mechanic Akin made up the crew. They kept bow from Lusaka airport, Zambia. The main cargo hold of the B737-200 Adv was crammed with Iranian cargo and the holds with our cargo.

I reported what had happened in Uganda and the condition of the Hercules, as well as Germam Holt's injuries. We kept south bow and prepared to cross Lake Edward. It would then fly another twenty nautical miles maintaining course, after turning and intercepting southeast bound and entering Rwandan airspace. He estimated arrival at the "Base of Operations" in four and a half hours, after landing to deliver our cargo.

The Commander Jean-Pierre estimated to arrive in Lusaka in one and a half hours and would try to contact us after their landing on the prearranged HF frequency.

As we entered Rwandan airspace, which was one of the worst in the world, we started our descent to land on a dirt road nine hundred meters long and perform the back-track over a cliff, as the road did not permit this manoeuvre. Of course, I did not expect a level grass field, this was not an airfield after all.

On crossing eight thousand feet I increased the rate of descent to start a spiral of three concentric circles and position myself at a short final. On passing three thousand feet I ordered the Landing Gear Down and Flap set for pitch.

A surface-to-air rocket went straight into the number two engine, exploding and tearing it off the wing, causing pieces to brutally hit the fuselage. The Hercules' lateral stability was compromised and it was prone to a dangerous low-altitude attitude and thick black smoke.

Germam Holt entered the cockpit and took up position in his seat. He immediately made emergency arrangements to avoid loss of fuel. Mark Kurt completed other emergency procedures and I controlled the Hercules to avoid loss of altitude and a dangerous attitude, when crossing one thousand five hundred feet another ground-to-air rocket was fired; that would be our death sentence, but I plunged the Hercules sharply towards the dirt runway with a high rate of descent as well as the speed to avoid impact. Mark Kurt, realising I was struggling to save us, commanded Full Flap Down to slow the landing speed. I crossed the "illusory headland" of the runway and once again forced the Hercules into another assault landing and then quickly commanded Speed Brake to avoid returning to flight. I quickly reversed the propellers of the external engines, avoiding the tendency to lose the axis of the narrow road. Once again a "cloud" of red dust covered the aircraft spectacularly.

The situation was precarious. The sequence of shots at the Hercules came from the left side of the road. No local defence was provided, so I managed to execute the back-track in an attempt to escape that hell. Luckily, the enemy infantry did not advance because they decided to attack with mortars. The customer gave no sign that he was willing to receive the package, and I did not know if we would get out alive that day. An aircraft is always a dangerous place. All it took was one mortar to hit the Hercules for the African continent to shudder with the explosion.

I decided to take some armaments from the client for our defence, with the help of all the crew members, while the mortars rushed closer and closer to the Hercules, which indicated that they were correcting their firing angle and that it would be hit at any moment. Everyone had their pistols in their waists and as a last resort, Germam Holt positioned himself together with Mabetu, and under the European's guidance, the African started firing the medium-range mortars. Mark Kurt and I, from another position, provided cover with our Belgian rifles. The confrontation had already lasted twenty minutes. The enemy's mortars were rushing closer and closer to the Hercules, when, contrary to our expectations, the client appeared in the opposite direction of the road at high speed with a truck and a jeep.

The truck stopped near the main loading door, and all the men quickly occupied the Hercules. Mark Kurt and I went towards the jeep, for, and after all, the package was not free. A nearly six-foot African was in charge and on seeing us said: "Brave ones! I want to see how you're going to get out of here." I wasted no time. I drew my forty-five-millimetre calibre pistol like lightning and, despite my five feet and forty-two inches, I pointed it at the arrogant man's head. He understood immediately and indicated where the payment was in the jeep. Mark Kurt checked the money as the mortar charge intensified, and closer and closer to the Hercules.

We moved away from the aircraft to avoid the worst, when a mortar hit the Hercules on the right wing and exploded, killing everyone inside and nearby, including the almost two-metre tall arrogant man. What was left was a jeep which became our means of escape.

Everyone knew the risks, including the client; after all, we were not playing at the naval battle. Germam Holt was wounded, we had no water or supplies, but we were well-armed. Survival in enemy terrain is based primarily on caution. No one is a friend, and everyone is a potential informer: simple villagers are capable of showing cooperation, and when you close your eyes you will never open them again.

The most important thing was to cross the border towards Zaire. The jeep had three quarters of its tank's fuel capacity, which allowed it to cover enough distance to reach the border. However, if it was necessary to refuel and we could not find one of those petrol stations anywhere on the road, we would abandon the jeep.

The daylight helped us to move along the road, but the lack of water was the most worrying thing, apart from the injured Germam Holt. I decided to drive at high speed, regardless of the fuel consumption. We found a stream and filled up the canteens. I left the jeep under a tree, taking advantage of the little shade. The extra tank of fuel contained a few litres; I poured it into the tank and went to the creek to wash it until I was sure it didn't have the smell of petrol. That tank became our water reservoir. I cleaned Germam Holt's wounds and applied fresh medical supplies to prevent infection: I asked the others to remove their t-shirts from under their shirts, wash them and hand them to me. I needed them dry to have to use on the German's wounds.

We needed rest. The place seemed appropriate for that. Resting doesn't exactly mean sleeping, but letting the adrenaline return to a normal state. The smell of blood can attract wild animals, among them the Savannah Hyena. They walk in packs, attack together, and that jaw is one of the most powerful in the animal world of that continent. When Africans see a Hyena, they never stand on a lower level than they do. The strategy is to stay on their feet, they feel insecure, yet avoiding them was still the best strategy.

When the B737-200 Adv returned to "Base of Operations", Jean-Pierre commented to Kruger on the in-flight contact between the aircraft and reported that after landing at Lusaka airport, he could not get a new contact via the HF frequency. They decided to wait for the Hercules to arrive at the "Base of Operations", and as time passed they realised that something had not gone right. Kruger took the initiative to fly the Hercules' return route with Bell UH-1. For this mission he ordered Full Tank and a one-hundred-litre tank on board the well-positioned and fixed helicopter, to avoid inconvenient movements to the stability of the aircraft.

Kruger left early in the morning with Patrick Singer and Hans Marzevic aboard the Bell UH-1 looking for us and heavily armed. I drove at night while my men slept. Sometimes Mabetu would wake up and talk to me and after a few minutes, I was cradled in the arms of Morpheus: the god of sleep from Greek mythology.

At dawn I realised that we were close to the border, I

accelerated and on a bend, I came across a border barrier improvised by Africans wielding their AK-47s towards the jeep. They opened fire. I immediately got down, took cover behind the jeep and shouted to Mabetu to get Germam Holt out of the vehicle. A shot hit Mark Kurt in the right thigh, but he bravely positioned himself, lying on the ground, and from under the jeep opened fire on them: the legs of the unfortunates were mercilessly sifted with Belgian projectiles, while the jeep received more than fifty shots. Mabetu prepared a Soviet RPG rocket launcher and handed it to Germam Holt to fire at the Rwandan soldiers' truck. Hitting it caused a spectacular explosion and intense fire accompanied by thick black smoke. The resistance we offered was up to our standard, however, the number of soldiers willing to face us was approximately sixty, and they were eager to capture and kill us.

We used everything we had at our disposal to face them, but we were surrounded. The amount of ammunition was not enough, and possibly the ones we had left would be those from our pistols for one last projectile against our own heads. Mabetu was wounded below the collarbone and in the left calf, yet my men were unwilling to surrender and continued to fight.

There were many dead and those that remained believed in capturing us. Until a morbid silence lingered on the African savannah. That silence was a harbinger of what was to come. I ordered my men to check their weaponry and prepare for man-to-man confrontation. I do not forget Mabetu's face as he dryly swallowed the dust and sweat that dripped down the skin of his face. I signalled to him with a closed fist indicating strength. Nothing happens by chance. That moment of the enemy regrouping was all the time we needed.

As the Rwandan soldiers rose towards us screaming, they

were silenced by the unmistakable thud of the clatter of propeller blades from the Bell UH-1, commanded by Kruger and with Patrick Singer firing his machine gun, thirty-millimetre calibre, at them. My eyes closed as a burst of machine-gun fire from Patrick Singer almost hit us, how close the enemy was to us. Those who were left fled. Patrick Singer and Hans Marzevic came down from the helicopter to rescue us.

We boarded the wounded first. There was no room for everyone in the helicopter because of the hundred-litre tank on board. Kruger ordered Patrick Singer to refuel the helicopter once more with Full Tank, while we took care of Mabetu, Germam Holt and Mark Kurt.

We remained at that location for another twenty-five minutes until we completed refuelling and left the one-hundred-litre barrel on the ground. One scene showed the hatred Patrick Singer felt: he went to each of the wounded and executed them without mercy.

Kruger took off with a bow from the "Base of Operations", including with our cash payment on board. The mercenary's motive is money; always has been and always will be. The landing at "Base of Operations" was technical due to a further refuelling to reach the Central Hospital in Kinshasa, where the wounded would be treated with all the care money could buy, as we had no tourist travel insurance.

Loyalty is priceless. Kruger knew exactly where to find us because he believed that, via the Hercules' return route, there was a chance, should the aircraft have made an emergency landing: the only road we would take to deliver our cargo would be the one towards the Zairean border. When Kruger saw the black smoke from the explosion of the truck on the horizon, the chances of finding us were good.

I reported to the Iranian the loss of the Hercules, and, as usual, his silence accompanied him in the hour of material loss. He did not resent it, but if there was one place that hurt more than a punch in the stomach it was his pocket, but he asked me why I was in Rwanda. Of course, I was waiting for the question. I answered coldly: "Business."

At that moment I realised that the Iranian knew that I was in Rwanda, because at no time did I mention that the loss of the Hercules had occurred in Rwanda, and, of course, there was a traitor among "my men".

Kruger took care of business and I took care of the schedule at our convenience, which was made public a few hours before the mission. I would find the traitor, that was a matter of honour for me. There is a saying: "Don't put off until tomorrow what can be done today."

I looked for Kruger and asked if he had noticed anything unusual during my absence. He replied: "No." I dismissed him, but when he headed for the door of the "Administration House", he stopped, as in a movie cliché, and turned his body slowly, facing me, and said: "Yes. I received a phone call asking if you were at the base. Obviously, I said: "No, of course not". I asked him if he recognised the voice. The answer was surprising: "It was Paul Levi."

If it was a matter of emergency or urgency, Paul Levi would have asked Kruger for help, as the German had the authority to do this in my absence. He did not justify to Kruger the reason for the call. He thought I would never return to the "Base of Operations", let alone come from the world of the dead.

Machiavelli the wise wrote: "Keep your enemy close so that you can watch him." Especially an Israeli ex-Mossad.

Chapter 10.

The bag with the payment for our cargo contained five hundred and eighty-five thousand dollars; this was the reason for the Rwandan soldiers being near the border with Zaire and putting a price on our heads. The bag with its precious contents was duly stowed and transported to one of the vaults in a bank in South Africa. My share was deposited in a bank account under a false name, but duly legal. The transfer to Enigma Enterprise in the Bahamas was guaranteed. I'm of Italian and French descent, nevertheless, I can be whoever I wish to be with the documents my British forger forges with unrivalled perfection.

The owner of Enigma Enterprise was an "Egyptian." He could sell to me, through my law firm, in which case I could choose the name and citizenship that suited me. In this world being a ghost is an art that starts from the ability to create enough illusion. The best for this is anonymity and being extremely discreet, something rare in the world of business and rich men. Forbes magazine says so!

There are three pieces of information of a human being that are unique: the well-known fingerprint, DNA and the iris of the eyes. As long as that was not a reality that interfered with my business, the world was mine.

My perception of reality and intuition started to become clearer than ever: those times were about to end. Why? Ten years had passed since my arrival in Zaire, and the African continent was entering a new phase after wars and more wars. Some European colonialist countries, as well as other countries with interests on the continent, began to re-approach the former colonies through powerful private and state companies presenting the most different proposals, such as the introduction of new telecommunication technology, opening up a portal to interact with the rest of the world, and this would lead them to ratings by international agencies at various levels and to financing from powerful banks in various deficit areas; the objective was to "invest". For all these wars were bad business for the companies and banks, not for the warlords.

Mercenaries will always exist, but like us, they never existed in Africa. Not that I wished to be recognised by the Guinness Book. My men had accumulated experience and a small fortune, under my responsibility, to start life anew. This was without counting the Boma mission. I did not involve a penny of each of them in my business dealings because I had the right to speculate with my capital, however, not with other people's capital. "Every rule has its exception, otherwise it becomes a law." I started with one hundred thousand dollars "borrowed" by the Iranian, of course, I did not keep the amount, however, I did not pay it back with interest. It is unchristian to charge and pay back with interest, according to Pope Innocent III, God rest his soul!

The recovery of my men at the hospital was like well-deserved "holidays", so to speak because they got away from that hellish life. Paul Levi and Babu returned on the seventh day, as in Genesis in the Bible, while I awaited an accurate account of the third raid on Boma, for I was ready to act like a guillotine.

I assembled them in the "Administration House". They both sat in the armchairs in front of my desk and I asked: "Well?"

Paul Levi gave as usual an explanation of the observations

and details, but this time he was careful to make his point about the security of the mining company and kept the suggestion of an attack in commando tactics. He also spoke of giving the men fifteen days of intense training directed at the objective. Despite the experience of my men, he considered it important to maintain the training and finally confirmed that the work on the airstrip was ready and no executive jet had landed during the observation period.

Babu agreed with his explanation, without adding any comment. Paul Levi suggested we pick a date to execute the mission in Boma. I looked into his blue eyes and said: "That I will determine in due course." The Israeli did not show any reaction in an attempt to maintain control, as he was trained to do by the Mossad.

Later that morning the access road to the "Base of Operations" showed a high volume of dust, due to the movement of heavy vehicles, under Tousset's orders, with fuel for the aircraft, diesel oil for the generator, petrol and supplies. But regardless of the routine supply of supplies, my orders were to maintain visual control over the men accompanying the convoy.

Tousset gave the routine orders to his subordinates and went to meet me at the "Administration House" to deliver the usual report of the total quantity of supplies supplied. I asked him to leave them on the table and offered him hot coffee. He accepted with a certain surprise and with a stupid smile, showing his teeth white as ivory. I handed him the mug with steaming coffee and we went to the balcony of the house. After tasting the coffee, he asked, "Has everything been going well, Captain?"

The silence lasted for a few seconds in the heat of the African savannah, and without taking my eyes off the horizon I replied, "Yes, everything in perfect order. Couldn't be better."

The Iranian's employee insisted on holding a dialogue with me, for surely there was some message from his employer between the lines. Tousset continued: "The boss is worried. He lost an expensive plane, that's bad for the boss's business. Don't you think so?"

I'm not a racist and never have been. With all the calmness in the world I replied: "I'll tell you something, mind your own business. You'll never be invited to your boss's party. You are nothing but a doormat where he wipes the soles of his shoes. Understand?"

Tousset had his pen in his mouth drinking coffee and choked, spitting out the precious liquid discovered by the Arabs. There was hatred on his face, to the point of losing control, but before he could rise, my pistol was pointed at his black face, full of restrained anger. I said to him: "Get out, you doormat; get out of here you arrogant bastard." Tousset turned away, muttering inaudible words between his teeth and stood next to his men, who were still working and took his anger out on them.

The message was given. The Iranian used Tousset to demonstrate his dissatisfaction with the loss of Hercules. I didn't mind, it was an occupational hazard. That aircraft had a terrible end, but she was part of the profits as well as the losses. It was more than paid for by the profit it had yielded to my men, and especially to me.

The heavy vehicles withdrew from the "Base of Operations" and disappeared along with Tousset. To our happiness, Akin called us for another lunch, gathering us all at the same table. I was in awe of the courage of my men and the respect they showed. During the meals, relaxed conversations between men from the same battlefield reigned supreme. I always remained observant and spoke little during the time I lived in the African savannah. After lunch, Paul Levi received my permission to tell the crew and mechanics about the training they would receive; the justification was to improve combat tactics.

Before my men left the mess hall after helping Akin with cleaning up, I ordered them to remain in the mess hall. There were the men who would form the Alpha and Bravo group for the mission in Boma and I told them: "We are about to execute an important mission. You must follow Paul Levi's instructions, without questioning what is required of you. Are we clear?"

The answer was a resounding: "Yes, sir."

The political situation in Zaire was beginning to show instability, and bad news is like gunpowder fuses: it runs rapidly in one direction only to end in an explosion with incalculable consequences. The president of Zaire at that time was Mobutu Sese Seko. His father was a cook for a Belgian judge in colonial times, who died before his son was born, and his mother died when he was eight years old. The wife of the Belgian judge took him in and taught him to speak, write and read in French.

The most striking characteristic of the young Mobutu was his rebelliousness. Despite having studied in a Catholic boarding school, he was sent by the priests to the army as punishment. The army is a disciplinarian and indoctrinator, and it was there that Mobutu found literature concerning Churchill, De Gaulle and Machiavelli. Who would have thought it? But what fascinated Mobutu was journalism, to the point that he abandoned the army and dedicated himself to his professional passion. And like a magnet, politics attracted him in 1956.

One of the men who stood out in politics in the Belgian Congo was Patrice Lumumba, an opponent of the Belgian colonialist regime and with pro-Soviet socialist thoughts. The anti-colonialist movement, combined with international pressure, forced Belgium to "grant" independence to the so-called Belgian Congo.

Mobutu was an advisor to Lumumba, but he was not pro-Soviet and even less a socialist. Belgian businessmen wanted at all costs a government aligned with the United States of America, stemming from the effect of the Cold War and territorial dispute for influence. They found a haven in Mobutu when they financed the coup in 1965. He handed Lumumba over to his enemies in Katanga province and they assassinated him.

One of Mobutu's first moves was to expel "Soviet advisers" from Congolese territory and demonstrate alignment with the United States of America in 1971 on a visit to President Richard Nixon. The Belgian Congo was renamed Zaire. Mobutu's politics were distinguished by corruption involving public money, with the acquiescence of France and the United States of America of the "Three Little Monkeys" type: don't see, don't hear and don't speak.

One of the countries that hosted Mobutu's fortune was Switzerland; through its exemplary banks, however, the international community knew where the money came from and how it was provided.

I watched very carefully what was happening in Mobutu's Zaire. If there is one thing that international relations appreciate it is the geopolitical value of a country. Zaire, with the end of the Cold War, lost importance in the balance of power of the Western superpowers in that part of Africa. Zaire was the counterpart of Angola, occupied by a socialist government under the tutelage of the USSR and Cuba. In my view, Mobutu was a card to be discarded from the deck, but not for democratic elections and so proffered by Western nations, but rather, for a war that was soon to break out. The fuse of gunpowder was already lit, the explosion would be a matter of time and the damage incalculable.

South Africa had been experiencing the end of the racist Apartheid regime since 1994, after the multiracial and democratic elections with victory for the African National Congress and Nelson Mandela. The winds in Africa were changing.

The training of my men was scheduled to start two days after our meeting in the mess hall. The overseas flights with the B707 and DC8 were maintained, and I interspersed the crew members on the flight schedules, as well as the deliveries of the Iranian's cargo, avoiding the suspicion of the novices, not included in the Boma mission. Kruger rescheduled some deliveries of our cargo, avoiding wear and tear and exposure. The focus shifted to the Boma mission.

The political instability in Zaire was clear, and the international community expected the worst since in Rwanda a tribal civil war was taking place, with the Hutu political elite using armed militias against the Tutsis, with genocidal consequences. The border of Zaire was taken over by hordes of fleeing Tutsis, something that had not yet been recorded by the international press.

I travelled from Kinshasa to Brussels for part of my men's training period, while Kruger remained in charge of the "Base of Operations" , and his brother, Kauffman, assisted him as his right-hand man. On arrival in Brussels, I phoned Desire and we met in a café near her work. Women are a gift from Olympus: the happy smile on her beautiful face matched her Chanel-cut hair. She, seeing me, ran up to me and received a small bouquet of red roses, nicely arranged by a florist near the café. She showed an infinite naivety, but also feminine sensuality.

We were chatting about various subjects that late afternoon

when she asked: "What do you want? Besides me, of course."

Without showing much interest in this important question, I disagreed, and after a few minutes, she insisted on the same question. Simply and objectively, I put the "cards on the table". She listened with interest and patience, and said, with sweet words on her lips: "Consider it done." I paid the bill and hand in hand we left like two teenagers in love and headed for the hotel where I was staying.

The next day I went to a stock brokerage indicated by my Jewish accountant, but he contacted me in advance to arrange the details with the owner to receive an important "Egyptian" businessman and demanded total professional secrecy.

Mr Sander received me at ten-thirty a.m. in his private office, showing good taste in his clothes and luxury in the furniture. He offered me coffee and Perrier mineral water. I accepted the kindness. After the courtesies, I went straight to the point and at 12:20 p.m. I left the head office of Mr Sander's brokerage firm with a youthful but restrained satisfaction, for there were still many details to be worked out. I went to a telephone box and completed a call to Cape Town. I remember that it didn't take long and when I finished I headed towards the hotel. I spent the afternoon beside the phone in my room waiting for a call.

The news from the African continent was not the best, especially from Zaire. The press and television began to highlight the human exodus from countries in armed conflict; no doubt arms trafficking was intense to meet the demand. The European stock markets showed some stability, yet the shares of certain companies in the areas of armed conflict were prone to severe instabilities and indicated dizzying falls. The basis of a company is production, and if it is unable to supply the market, the commercial value goes down, as do the shares traded on the world's stock exchanges.

The hotel room phone rang. I let it ring until the third time, as agreed, and answered it. I listened to every word and hung up. I was calm and composed, without any reaction to the call. It was a risky move.

I took the opportunity to take a long shower and shave. In the bathroom, I could look into my eyes and see myself, something uncommon to ordinary men. At 17:05 Desire called my room and we arranged to meet at the hotel bar. I saw her arrive in an elegant dress, wearing high shoes, on her forearm a simple coat and in her right hand a short strap bag. The earrings matched the colour of her eyes, and the lipstick further highlighted her feminine beauty. I was not a man to fall in love; there would be plenty of time to find a woman reliable enough to confess every minute of my life.

Desire's casualness made those minutes priceless. She mastered the art of charm through the combination of beauty and sympathy, capable of transforming any environment. Some men looked at her and desired her, but I don't think she would allow any of them to make a joke, because she seemed selective and predatory. I did not ask about what I had exposed her to at the café the previous afternoon, however, after I asked the waiter for a bottle of the splendid French wine, *Vosne Romanée by J. Bouchard*, she propped her right elbow on the table for two, and with her delicate hand below her chin said: "Here is what you asked for." She withdrew from her small handbag a small envelope and placed it on the table. With the index finger of her left hand, she pushed it towards me and gave a subtle smile of a passionate kitten.

I kept the small envelope in the pocket of my blazer. The waiter brought the bottle of wine and opened it with all the prized ritual, allowing us the vice of Bacchus. We remained for two and a half hours chatting in a relaxed way. For her time did not exist.

That night, in my room, we had unforgettable moments. I left the next morning for London, without first leaving in her small purse a signed cheque for an amount in Belgian Francs that would allow her to live comfortably for many years, provided she knew how to invest it. Desire was not, and never has been a luxury prostitute, but one of the many links I have built to achieve my goals. She lives in Florence, Italy, and knew how to invest every penny. We are great friends today.

When I arrived at London airport, a private limousine with a chauffeur was waiting for me. The driver was a white-haired gentleman of British nationality and from our first contact showed himself to be discreet. The records informed us that he was a military man, the highest rank he had reached: Sergeant Major, with some honours and medals, a widower with two married children. Besides being discreet, he knew how to conduct himself politely; in his gaze there was serenity and no ambition.

My driver's name was Gregory. He opened the back door on the left side gently without taking his eyes off the movement of people behind my back. When I got inside the comfortable car, there were two London tabloids positioned in front of me: one business and one news.

On the second, and the front page: the political crisis in Zaire. I put that newspaper aside and opened the business one in search of the stock market indicators and certain stocks. And once again my cynical smile showed on my face.

Gregory drove the comfortable automobile to my law office. Yes, I owned a powerful but not eccentric law firm, which handled the legalisation of my "investments". It is not what you think! It's not money laundering. It's legalising businesses under the legitimate eye of the law; it doesn't mean that the capital is inside the company's vault. The time of walking into a bank with a suitcase full of money and depositing it without question was about to end.

Believe it! A bank takes your hard-earned money and turns it into negotiable papers, gold, loans of all kinds and everything that has future value; while you receive a bank statement with "positive credit". If you and all the account holders go to the bank on the same day and decide to withdraw all the money that each one has as "positive credit", the bank immediately files for bankruptcy. Where is your hard-earned "positive credit"? Excuse me, you have no idea. Or do you?

Technology was indicating back then in which direction mankind was heading in a senseless direction, and in my view, many things were about to change. I was right, again.

I never liked lengthy meetings, and so it was that day in my London law office. On my desk were three folders with previously set documents. Sitting at the table were five lawyers, "created snakes" in tax taxation, international financial markets, business administration, political economy and international law. I did not need truculence, but rather lawyers capable of defending my "financial territoriality" and, above all, what was to come. The small envelope delivered by the beautiful Desire, I passed it on to the care of my lawyers.

I called Mr Sander and ordered another bold move. He did not contest me, knowing that in less than twenty-four hours my initial card had surprised him. From his experience, he realised that I dealt with the cards, which did not mean that they were marked cards, for, in this case, it was pure intuition, observation of reality and luck. I waited until Mr Sander answered me: "It's done. May God help us."

I waited a few seconds and then I answered: "Thank you. We'll talk soon."

Chapter 11.

I left London that night bound for Kinshasa. And as usual, Babu was waiting for me at the airport exit. It was noticeable the movement of soldiers from Mobutu's army, as well as the political instability. Reading a British tabloid was nothing compared to living those days in Africa, especially in Zaire. My faithful African friend told me that the training of my men was going well and that Paul Levi was committed to preparing them. Babu's words matched the conversation I had with Kruger and Kauffman when I arrived at the "Base of Operations".

I tasked Babu to prepare the Mig-8 helicopter that was still hidden and to check the Bell UH-1. The next day I followed the training of my men: there was no doubt that they were prepared. We gathered under the shade of the wing of one of the Hercules. Everyone was sitting on the ground while Paul Levi and I remained standing. I did not intend to make a motivational speech, but my men placed in me the hope of leaving the African hell, and that was my intention and I would only do so with the full boot of war. My words were: "Thank you for committing yourselves and cooperating with the instruction. I understand that you are prepared and don't think it'll be easy. You'll be informed when we leave."

What I noticed in their eyes was something dangerous: "The illusion of hope." There were determination and courage in carrying out the mission in Boma, and that was enough.

On 26 November 1996, we watched on television the final of the Toyota Cup in the Olympic Stadium in Tokyo, Japan, between two great football teams: Juventus from Italy and River Plate from Argentina. And to my delight, Juventus won 1-0, with a goal by Del Pietro in the eighty-first minute. After watching the football match, I ordered Paul Levi to keep on training, improving the combat tactics, including the melee ones. According to my calculations, time was in my favour and I wanted my men in a perfect state of alert for the combat.

I followed everything that was happening at the "Base of Operations" and it caught my attention that they hadn't received another shipment of aviation fuel; that didn't mean there wasn't enough for four months. In my view, it was another suspicion of the foreshadowing of the unsustainable political situation in Mobutu's Zaire. The biggest opponent of Mobutu's dictatorship was the guerrilla Joseph Kabila, who was imposing defeats on Zaire's central government army. And to succeed he needed: money, men and weapons. Who was financing Kabila?

My contact with the outside world was not restricted. I sent direct orders to Mr Sander and my law office in London. In the first week of December 1996, I sent a telegram to my gunsmith: to prepare his son Mpumelele to travel and to arrange the exchange with his brother who lived with his mother.

Two days after sending the telegram I took off for South Africa. On the return flight, Mpumelele was on board the B737-200 Adv as part of the crew and with him two canvas bags.

I remember; I asked: "What's in those bags?"

He replied: "Those are my girls."

At the moment I was startled, but he was referring to the machinery for opening the safe. On one of the flights from Europe, I smuggled in one hundred kilos of explosive with high demolition power and ten kilos of C4 explosive for restricted military use. On my last trip to London, I took the opportunity to buy three high-quality military field bags made of waterproof fabric, which I brought in my suitcase.

On December 24, 1996, I ordered Akin to prepare a special meal, as the Christians were celebrating the birth of the son of God, and since almost everyone was Christian, nothing could be more fitting than for them to celebrate, including the Israeli and Jewish Paul Levi; after all, Jesus Christ was Jewish.

That was not the last meal of those condemned to death, however, it was a moment when men tried to strive for a reunion with their being. That is to say: to reflect on life, including finding the motivation to survive and to see their relatives again. For that, they had to fight like gladiators in the arena of the Coliseum. And that moment was closer than they imagined.

The only ones who did not attend the supper were the rookies, as the overseas flight schedule was designed to get them away from the "Base of Operations". When the B707 and DC8 took off in the early afternoon of 24 December 1996, bound for Europe and scheduled to return on 27 December 1996, they knew absolutely nothing of our intentions.

In the early hours of 25 December 1996, we filled up one of the Hercules with Full Tanks and made it ready for any emergency. The Mig-8 was carefully towed away and, to my surprise, the mechanics painted it black like the other helicopter. Kauffman started the imposing Soviet helicopter and Kruger the Bell UH-1.

Despite the special meal prepared by Akin, I did not allow any alcoholic drinks as a precaution. The fuelling of the helicopters indicated to my men that we would be going into action. The explosives and armaments were housed in the cargo compartment of each helicopter, and when everything was ready I ordered everyone to go to the mess hall, where a reinforced breakfast was waiting for them. It was four a.m. on December 25, 1996.

While the rest of the men were in the mess hall, I called Commander Jean-Pierre, his brother Co-pilot Jean-Batiste, Flight Engineer Alan Palmer and Master Loader and mechanic Akin for a special mission. Commander Jean-Pierre would take off the Hercules after the second helicopter took off. He would stay away to the West of Boma at approximately ten nautical miles, hold on to FL050, await contact via VHF and if necessary make an assault landing on the mining company's airstrip. I gave him a map with the details of a possible landing approach.

I returned to the dining room and opened the detailed map of the region: from that moment on the "Boma Mission" was underway.

The ten-man Alpha group: Kauffman as pilot of the Mig-8, John Brooks, Douglas, Joseph Marcos, Lee, Patrick Singer, Hans Marzevic, Mabetu, Gustav and Nikolij were all armed to the teeth, including RPG rockets and thirty-millimetre calibre machine guns. The Mig-8 would take off first, approach the mining company, land on the highest part of the building with predetermined landing objectives of the first assault command and immediately destroy the two watchtowers with RPG rockets, take the attack position eliminating all resistance to maintain a secure perimeter, besides destroying any moving or occupied vehicle by the enemy and imposing terror and fear. No member of the Alpha group should enter the building.

Bravo group was formed by seven men: Kruger as pilot of the Bell UH-1, Babu, Paul Levi, Mpumelele, Germam Holt and Mark Kurt and myself. Our firepower was similar to that of the

Alpha group, however, Babu and Paul Levi would escort and protect Mpumelele, for without him the opening of the vault would be compromised. The Bell UH-1 would take off five minutes after the Mig-8; that was the time they had until our landing arrival in the parking yard in front of the building's entrance. The Alpha group, with a vantage position at the highest point, would eliminate the initial resistance.

In my men's eyes, there was euphoria and good humour. I ordered both helicopters to leave the combat sector and stay away, hovering and awaiting contact via VHF radio on a secret frequency between the helicopter pilots and the Hercules. I carried with me a portable radio communicator with Swedish VHF frequencies bought in Belgium, something that surprised Paul Levi.

My Swiss Universal Genève watch, a gift from my father, indicated five-fifteen a.m. I ordered everyone to adjust their watches and each group to go to their respective helicopter. Before boarding we greeted each other, knowing the dangers we were prepared to face.

Kauffman started the Mig-8 engine and the main rotor blades started spinning in sync with the tail rotor blades. The German was very particular and suggested keeping the anti-collision lamp and the navigation lamps off to avoid detection; this was defined in agreement with his brother, Kruger. The smell of burning paraffin was intense while we waited for the Soviet helicopter to start its flight. Kauffman made a positive sign with the thumb of his right hand.

The Mig-8 was heavy and began to lift off the ground with the force of Atlas; that Soviet machine was spectacular. Kauffman made the Soviet monster lift-off for good, gaining height and horizontal speed. The men on board howled, and the

Mig-8 moved off in the capture of Boma's bow already at flying altitude.

We waited the agreed time as Kruger started the engine start of the Bell UH-1. We were all on board and ready. The German cheerfully commanded the collective and accelerated the engine. The main rotor blades increased the rotation, keeping the unmistakable sound of that war machine. At that moment we left the "Base of Operations". Next to us, the four Hercules crew members nodded in agreement and headed in the direction of the aircraft for take-off.

The approach of the Mig-8 took place with precision over the flat roof of the highest point of the mining building. Hans Marzevic was the first to leave the helicopter and positioned himself with the Soviet RPG rocket launcher aimed at the south sector tower and Joseph Marcos was the second to land and immediately aimed the Soviet RPG rocket launcher at the opposite tower. Together, they fired. The first enemy casualties occurred with the destruction of the watchtowers, with columns of smoke immediately appearing from the explosions. When all the men were in position, Kauffman took off once more with the Mig-8 and moved away as planned.

The security alarm was triggered. Rushing and desperation took over the emotions of each of them, and those who dared to wield weapons were felled with precise shots. From inside the building, through a side door, other security guards came out, with Belgian-made military FAL rifles, trying to position themselves in search of my men. The resistance was inferior to our firepower, and we had the advantage of dominating the highest point. Then the Bell UH-1 came up from the eastern sector, at high speed to reach the landing point in the car park.

The security guards realised that a new landing would put

the resistance in check; they dared to aim a bazooka at the Bell UH-1. Then Kruger shouted, "Germam, shoot with everything." The skilled German quickly turned the helicopter around and his compatriot Germam Holt opened fire with his machine gun, thirty-millimetre calibre, sieving and tearing the upper torso off the security guard, although the unfortunate man inadvertently fired, but without hitting us.

Kruger immediately landed the Bell UH-1 under a hail of FAL fire from the security guards, but we managed to disembark and quickly threw ourselves to the ground as Mark Kurt and Germam Holt began firing shots at the security guards; I saw many get hit as Babu and Paul Levi looked after Mpumelele. The men of the Alpha group were concentrating their fire in front of the building, providing cover. At that moment I realised we should move forward and we ran towards the entrance when we were met by a group from inside the building. Germam Holt prepared the rocket launcher and fired mercilessly, followed by an explosion that shook the entrance, besides causing a lot of fire and smoke. We tried to advance. I saw a security guard aiming at one of us and then his head ricocheted off a shot coming from a member of the Alpha group.

I looked at the northeast sector and saw the two helicopters hovering at approximately the agreed altitude, which indicated that there was possibly no air defence plan from the mining company's security guards. I decided we would move in at that point. The sight of the two helicopters hovering was the last image I had before entering the building. What followed was a fierce fight, corridor by corridor. We used every type of weapon available to eliminate the defence of the security guards as we approached the vault sector.

I believed that with the tactic of terrorising the enemy they would surrender. I had Paul Levi prepare a demolishing charge against what I considered to be their last resistance. The explosion silenced the building, which was felt throughout the structure, with fatal consequences for those who tried to defend another's property.

None of us were injured. As I passed through the area of the explosion I saw men without trunks and others without the slightest possibility of identification, not to mention the smell of burnt human flesh. There is no difference in the smell of burnt human flesh from a white man or a black man. We were mercenaries bent on robbing the mining company, and anyone who stood in our way would not survive another day.

Finally, we were facing the door of the Fabergé vault. I ordered Germam Holt and Mark Kurt to remain in a defensive position and shoot down anyone who appeared in front of them. Mpumelele more than quickly pulled out his bags, which he called 'his girls', and with all the mastery of one who knows what he is doing set to work. Paul Levi looked at Mpumelele, and in his eyes, there was no doubt that the boy would open the safe. It was twenty-three minutes of anxiety not shown by me, but I confess I was waiting to hear the sweet sound of the door opening.

Mpumelele looked at me and said: "Captain, you are ready. Will you do the honours of opening it, sir?"

I slung my rifle to my back, put both hands to command the roundabout lever and finally made enough force to unlock, "It made the light".

I was the first to enter the vault and there were exposed the most precious and valuables stones in the world. I did not let myself be taken by emotion and I ordered Babu, Mpumelele and Paul Levi to enter, without first handing them the bags that I had brought with me and I said, "Do not leave any behind to tell the story," and in a few minutes we left the vault, and under the escort of the Bravo group I went towards the entrance. I heard some shots, but everything was under control. When I arrived near the entrance I saw the tunnel that connected to the mine and stopped observing.

Kruger landed the Bell UH-1 in the car park after contacting him through the VHF radio. I ordered Babu and Germam Holt to bring the rest of the high explosive and the C4. I decided to blow up the mine entrance and the high-tech machinery brought from Tripoli. I could not waste much time, as I did not know if there was still any response power from any support point. The recommended thing was to leave the place as soon as possible, and at that moment Paul Levi offered to accompany me to the mine and help with the explosives. For the first time I saw fear in Babu's eyes, and to his surprise, I answered the Israeli: "Yes. Your help is always welcome."

My men helped us with the transport of the explosives and I ordered them to return; I handed Babu the VHF radio. His hands were shaking and showing fear once again. To calm him down I said: "Go calmly, in a while we will have a beer together." Everyone left, and the Israeli and I remained there.

We took care of all the details so that the mine and the machinery would remain closed and inoperative for a good while. Paul Levi knew what he was doing; he was impeccable.

I asked bluntly and unexpectedly, "How long have you been working for the Iranian?"

The ex-Mossad replied, "A long time. That's not news to you." We stood five feet away from each other, face to face.

And I said, "You knew that one day we would face each other. I know you're a traitor."

I have never fought an Israeli, an ex-Mossad. He pulled out a knife from the back of his leather belt and stood there like an elite soldier, ready to face me. Paul Levi was a difficult opponent and I had no choice but to assume the combat position, wait for his attacks and let him wear himself out to the point of beating him intelligently. It was more than fifteen minutes of attempts of one killing the other. I wished to give him a quick death.

The Israeli was demonstrating to lose self-control, as he was beginning to exhaust his tricks, already known to me for a long time. When I least expected it I blocked a standing blow with my forearm and spun him around with no possibility of defence. His back snapped close to my chest, with my arm price to his neck and without wasting any time I landed a top to bottom blow with all my might, going through his sternum to the stop of the combat knife. Paul Levi was dead and I dropped him to the dusty ground. Behind me stood Babu, bug-eyed, Germam Holt and Mark Kurt, who had watched the last moments of the combat between two mercenaries. Our difference was in character; betrayal among mercenaries is unforgivable and is paid for with one's life.

I ordered them to leave the place in the direction of the entrance. Babu carried the spool of wires and connected them to the terminals, awaiting my final order. He commanded the device with determination. The explosion was violent enough to collapse almost a hundred meters of the ceiling between the tunnel and the mine, turning the traitor's body into dust. I remember my words after the explosion: "From dust, you came to dust you shall return."

A familiar voice called out over the VHF radio; it was Kauffman. He warned us that government troops were moving along the only road in three trucks, a jeep and a light armoured car with a one hundred and five-millimetre calibre cannon, in the direction of the Belgique Minère building, trying to frustrate our escape. I had not counted on a confrontation with government troops and had no interest in being identified: we had left no survivors of the Sécurité des Biens to tell the story. I ordered Kauffman to land the Mig-8 next to the Bell UH-1 to leave the scene immediately.

Two of my men were slightly wounded: Gustav in the right leg and Lee below the left hip. When they were ready, I ordered them to take off in the opposite direction from the "Base of Operations" in a low flight over the Congo River; with sufficient distance to avoid being detected and identified by government troops.

After sufficient distance, both helicopters turned around opening an arc to intercept the definitive bow of "our home in Africa". Before leaving the Belgique Minère building, my faithful African friend Babu left written on one of the outside walls: "Souvenirs de Kabila", about the Congolese guerrilla and staunch opponent of Mobutu.

The Hercules commanded by Jean-Pierre landed at the Base of Operations twenty minutes after our arrival and as soon as it parked in the courtyard in front of the hangar, without turning off the four powerful engines, the main cargo door was opened by Akin and the traction cable was hooked to the Mig-8.

Akin closed the main cargo door, and Jean-Pierre taxied the Hercules to the headland, lined it up and took off immediately. The Mig-8 was launched from five thousand feet over Angolan territory. There was nothing left after the explosion because of the impact against the ground.

The B737-200 Adv was refuelled and prepared for a flight to Cape Town. The charter flight plan was approved in advance by the country's aviation authority. On 25 December 1996, I took off with three bags full of the world's most valuable diamonds. Not before the B737-200 Adv was registered by a traditional European commercial company, and painted under total secrecy by my mechanics, two days before the "Mission of Boma". My crew consisted of Mark Kurt, Babu and Mpumelele. All dressed as commercial airline pilots: caps, blazers with their respective insignia, ties, wings on their shirts and briefcases.

Before leaving for South Africa, I called Mr Sander in Brussels and ordered him to carry out the financial operations as agreed for 26 December 1996. He asked me: "How do you manage to be so cold-blooded in business?"

My answer was a single word, "Intuition," and I hung up with a cynical smile, without singing victory.

A company specialising in the reception and dispatch of charter flights in Cape Town was contracted by my company to handle our flight; all with management from my Jewish accountant. Our briefcases contained the diamonds. We were conducted to have our documents checked by the South African border authority, have no doubt, our passports were fake, as were the stamps from various countries of entry as crew members, which was common and very welcome by the entry permits in various countries. None of us were questioned and the "welcome to South Africa" was the "password" that everything was in perfect order as we commented on their football team, something pleasing to the South African people. So, we praised the result of South Africa, which won the Nations Championship 2-0 against Tunisia.

And believe me: we all got through without our bags being searched. On the faces of the South Africans was stamped the pride of being the 1996 champions of Mama Africa, but before we left "in freedom" I looked back over my right shoulder through my dark pilot glasses and said: "You will always be the best, believe that. I love all of this. I love Mama Africa."

The South Africans melted at that flattering comment. One of them said: "Commander, you are great."

After exchanging pleasantries, we left the airport and boarded a chauffeur-driven vehicle hired by my accountant and headed towards the hotel. The reservation was for three single rooms as Mpumelele was expected by his father in the hotel lobby. Inside the vehicle, I handed my gunsmith's son an envelope containing five thousand US dollars and said: "This is a gift. Don't go out spending it on futilities and avoid drawing attention to yourself. Are we clear?" Mpumelele received the envelope and tucked it inside the inside pocket of his blazer after shaking my hand in gratitude for the trust placed in him.

In the hotel hall, my gunsmith was waiting for us sitting cross-legged and quietly reading the newspaper. He reminded me of the American actor Morgan Freeman. When he saw me he stood up and walked towards me, his eyes full of pride for his son's work. He greeted me with an intense handshake, and I said to him: "Your boy has behaved like a great professional. He has my admiration for the courage he has shown." I saw for the first time my gunsmith's eyes with tears, even though we were mercenaries and he had an outlaw son. Many men in expensive suits and fancy ties are worse than a safecracker, and yet they are not hated by the plebs.

That Wednesday, December 25, 1996, the day was notoriously intense. The gunsmith and his son left. Of course, the payment of five hundred thousand dollars would do it to the gunsmith without the South African authorities being suspicious, for he knew with whom he was dealing. Babu and Mark Kurt slept the rest of the day and we met again only for dinner, and without any kind of fuss. We kept our posture as ordinary crew members.

The next day, after breakfast, my Jewish accountant was in the hotel lobby waiting. With him was a bag and inside it two more similar to the ones I had bought in Belgium. We went up the lift to the floor of our rooms, and Babu and Mark Kurt brought the briefcases, and, with great care, we transferred the diamonds into the three pouches. I ordered the counter to come down and wait for us in front of the hotel exit, ready to leave.

We used the stairs to reach the hall, however, each of us left for the car with an interval of fifteen seconds. At the wheel was the Jewish accountant. When he saw me, I gestured for him to leave the wheel with me. Like lightning, I was behind the wheel of an automatic Mercedes Benz. After eight minutes of driving, I pulled into the bank's car park to deposit the diamonds in fifteen rented boxes, under the custody of the bank.

The white South African manager knew me and was waiting with all the insurance papers for the contents to be deposited. My lawyers had lined everything up in advance.

The emerald gleam of his green eyes, upon seeing me, opened a smile of satisfaction on my lips; I knew the "quality" of the client who had just entered the branch. In business, whatever it may be, one should not leave "loose ends": every detail counts.

They stayed in a VIP room next to the three bags full of diamonds and enjoyed some of the treats that the bank provided, without excess, to clients of that level. I signed papers to gain access to the tellers. In that same bank, I kept two bank accounts. There is a very important principle to avoid losses: "Never put all your eggs in one basket."

The capital of each of my men, coming from the carga nostra, I kept in another bank. When the banking bureaucracy was over, the manager led me into a room and from there to the safe. Guess which one was the manufacturer? Exactly, it was a state-of-the-art Fabergé. My attention was drawn to the electronic device to open and close it, which did not exist in the Fabergé broken into by Mpumelele. But what did that matter now?

Babu and Mark Kurt brought the three bags, but they could not go beyond that point, as only the customer had access. They withdrew and went back to the VIP room. I went to all the trouble of packing the "arsenal of diamonds" into the fifteen boxes.

This was another step towards my goals. And without any ridiculous emotion in front of the power that those wonderful and natural stones exerted in the eyes of men, I deposited them, closed each box and kept the keys.

I thanked the manager for all his attention and we said goodbye. As I entered the Jewish accountant's car I said to him: "Let's go to the other bank now." When the car was parked near the building, I ordered them to stay inside and wait. In possession of the keys to the boxes, I went on foot to the workshop of a master key-maker and had exact copies made of each one. Inside the bank, the manager was talking to her boss. When she finished, she went to meet me. After the formal greetings, I asked to access one of the boxes she kept in the bank. She promptly led me to the place and I was in total privacy. I opened the chosen box and deposited the copies of the keys; it was a back-up in case of emergency.

I left the bank, looked for a public telephone and made a call to Mr Sander in Brussels. After identifying myself, I asked: "Everything in order?"

Mr Sander answered: "Yes, everything as you ordered," and he added: "If you allow me, it was a perfect move. How did you know?"

205

I replied: "Luck, pure luck, Mr Sander."

My Jewish accountant brought us back to the hotel and said goodbye, but I alerted him to take all actions to facilitate the return of the B737-200 Adv to the "Base of Operations", starting with cancelling the charter flight with the South African aviation authority and requesting an international transfer flight with the company that had received us at Cape Town airport. We departed with the B737-200 Adv towards "Base of Operations" in the early hours of the next day. On the faces of my crew, there was satisfaction at the outcome of the mission accomplished.

Mark Kurt made contact with our communications tower, where Akin was waiting for us, and then I initiated a right turn at a thirty-degree inclination in order to intercept the axis of the runway and commanded: Landing Gear Down, however, the Nose Gear did not indicate lowered and locked. We were two miles from the headland, lining up with the axis of the runway. I ordered "Go-around" and symmetrical power from both engines and compatible with the requirement. This meant a forward thrust maintaining the axis of the runway and with Flap confirmed in the appropriate position for the procedure, when I heard Mark Kurt confirm: "Positive Rate of Climb", then I ordered: "Gear Up".

Babu was in the observer's centre seat and had never seen that procedure in the cockpit. My faithful African friend's hands were like cat's nails digging into my seat. Despite the darkness of the night, Akin could tell by the headlights that the B737-200 Adv was changing position relative to the ground, which indicated a change in flight attitude. Mark Kurt calmed him down, informing him of the approach. I stabilised the aircraft at FL050 with compatible speed and ordered Mark Kurt to check the *Emergency Manual* for partial landing gear harnessing, in this case, the nose gear.

Apart from knowledge of piloting technique, aircraft model characteristics and systems, which made conducting an emergency safe, was a new concept in world aviation called: "Cabin Coordination". We were not commercial airline pilots with annual training in flight simulators, medical examinations and everything that covers a pilot with aura. All we had to do was follow what the manufacturer wrote in the manual.

I have always kept two maxims for a pilot: the first: "In an emergency, be calm, elegant and tranquil"; the second, as a doctrinal rule: "A pilot must have discipline, doctrine and humility. The whole debate ends in the manual. God exists and none of us is Him."

Mark Kurt, having found the procedure, asked: "Can we start reading the procedures for manually lowering the nose gear?"

I replied: "We have enough fuel on board. How about trying to lower it normally?"

He agreed and alerted Akin that we were starting our descent, again a right turn, but with low pitch until we reached the base leg of the approach procedure. With Flap at twenty-five degrees, I ordered: Landing Gear Down. The lever was lowered to the Down position, while Mark Kurt followed the traffic of the down and locked indicator lights. And to Babu's relief, we heard: "Tree Green Lights, Gear Down and Blocked."

I crossed the head of the runway, lit by Akin from the communications tower, and made a smooth landing. During taxi, I ordered Babu to have the B737-200 Adv towed into the hangar, then remove the current paint and place it on the hydraulic jacks to check the landing gear, as possibly the climb and harness sequence valve was failing intermittently, however, this was a maintenance matter only, as I had other matters to attend to and that day the B707 and DC8 would be returning from Europe.

Chapter 12.

The news circulating in the newspapers indicated the advance of Kabila's guerrilla troops. At this rate, the seizure of power would be a matter of months. One of the pro-Mobutu newspapers "leaked" the news of the attack on the Belgique Minèire and the death of the security guards of the Sécurité des Biens company. Kabila was blamed for the criminal attack, and the African and international community tried to repudiate it.

That news reached Brussels, and Mr Sander knew exactly what to do. My law firm handled every legal detail with the precision of a Swiss watch.

On the afternoon of December 27, 1996, I gathered my men in the cafeteria after lunch and thanked each one with a handshake for their courage, loyalty and respect. Words encourage the human being, but what they wanted was to know the "bottom line". I said: "Soon we must leave this place, and each one of you will leave as a millionaire. I hope you know how to make the most of every penny." For the first time I saw them happy that they were free from the African Hell, yet we had to wait for some political events to come. They knew that secrecy was important until they received the war boot, because from then on everyone would be on their own.

Before the end of 1996, I ordered Kruger to suspend all purchases and sales of our cargo, limiting us to a few scarce flights due to the instability in the region. I saw the opportunity to recommend to the Iranian to transfer the aircraft to Tunisia or Morocco and definitively abandon the "Base of Operations" until the political and economic situation in Zaire was defined.

Wounded pride is something we cannot measure in every human being. For him, withdrawing from Zaire meant losing a business of incalculable proportions. He believed that everything would continue as it was and in Mobutu's hands. The Iranian had the right to believe what he wished, but the reality at the end of 1996 indicated Kabila's victory soon. On 4 April 1997 all the Iranian's aircraft took off for Rabat and curiously, on 5 April 1997, a violent bombardment by the Zairean Air Force took place against the "Base of Operations", including against the airstrip. I learned that there were three hours of attacks against an inert target that offered no resistance whatsoever. The remaining fuel tank burned for two and a half days, and the fire consumed the accommodation, mess hall and hangar. No stone was left unturned.

The Bell UH-1 helicopter was loaded onto one of the Hercules, and I shipped it via cargo ship to the port of Cardiff, UK, using my company in South Africa as the rightful owner. Within three months the process was legalised by my law firm, which received final registration. To this day I keep that helicopter as a trophy from that time, but I dare not fly helicopters, however, I never liked rotary wings.

Before we left for Rabat, I once again gathered my men and informed them that they would all receive legitimate documents to enter their countries and that all criminal proceedings were extinct, which is like saying and as I promised: "They would be free men." Everything was handled by my law firm in London, and I charged absolutely nothing.

In May 1997, the government of the dictator Mobutu was

defeated by Kabila's guerrillas when they took the capital Kinshasa; and Mobutu had no choice but to leave Zaire and go into exile in Rabat. However, he carried an incalculable fortune in his private B707, in addition to sums accumulated in Swiss banks that exceeded the total value of Zaire's foreign debt. Mobutu died on 7 September 1997 in Rabat.

The new government of the former Belgian Congo was headed by Kabila, and one of the first acts was to rename the country: the Democratic Republic of Congo. My grandfather once said: "A man should not stand on the fence, for he will be stoned by both neighbours." For a mercenary, there is no side but money, no ideal but reality, no good or bad side. A mercenary is like a one-sided coin.

I financed Kabila against Mobutu's dictatorial regime with modern weaponry and ammunition of all kinds, for he was one of my future bets to take possession of what was mine.

My men left for their home countries in August 1997. Each one signed a "silence pact" for twenty years straight to keep secret everything that had occurred at that time, including the equitable millionaire sum that each one received in a private bank account in Switzerland. You can't buy silence from those who have: eyes, ears and mouth with tongue. We were mercenaries, but there is a code among this species of men that goes beyond the capacity of understanding and the eyes of ordinary men. And in that sense, the pact of silence was one more guarantee of how one could penalise any one of us.

I left Rabat on 1 September 1997 for Lisbon with a connection to London, obviously after handing over the Iranian aircraft under my responsibility to his emissary, whose name was Al Marak and who called himself an aircraft maintenance technician. It didn't matter to me whether he was the Caliph of

Baghdad or whoever he wanted to be.

My flight from Rabat was delayed by almost an hour. Immediately, however, and absolutely, a new life in a new identity began for me. But my men would always remember me as Captain. The bet to find out my country of origin was without a winner, at least until they left for their home countries.

On arrival in London, my driver Gregory was waiting for me at the Heathrow airport exit. He very politely said: "You look tired, sir."

I immediately replied: "You have no idea."

My flat in London was extremely comfortable. I remember that I asked Gregory not to be disturbed for two days in a row, but I did not waste time with trivial matters. The next day I surprised Gregory with the request to take me to my law office. When I got there I could see the documents that made me the absolute owner of Belgique Minèire and the insurance that the company had received from the security and insurance company Sécurité des Biens.

The contracted policy obliged the company Sécurité des Biens to pay for the damage that had occurred. I received the amount through my law office in London and allocated thirty-five per cent of the amount received to all the families of the security guards killed in the armed conflict, as the life insurance for each one of those souls was only five thousand US dollars. Insufficient to attend to the orphaned children and widowed wives. Because of their irresponsibility in defending the good of others, I had to take this decision, demonstrating that my administration "had nothing to do with what happened" that day. The rest of the amount received was waiting in a bank account to be destined for the reconstruction of the building's infrastructure and reactivation of the mine.

In June 1998, negotiations with Kabila's government began in Paris. I had an "invoice" to collect. After all, as the Americans say: "There's no such thing as free food." Have no doubt, it was a marked card negotiation because the aim was to demonstrate to public opinion that: "who was now in charge in the Democratic Republic of Congo" was Kabila.

In a few months, the French engineers had reconstructed the damaged parts of the building, using the side and façade plans that I had. They created new sectors for geological research and studies. I imported high-precision machinery and employed natives for the extraction of the best diamond in the world. The most difficult job was to remove the debris of almost a hundred linear metres from the tunnel and the mine entrance and within a week I was informed that I was guaranteed main access to the largest diamond deposit ever seen.

Belgique Minèire went into full swing at the end of 1998, but ambition is a very dangerous thing when you have no control over it. Kabila was receiving dividends in his Swiss bank account. As you can see: "The dog has changed, but the collar is the same." What was treated with me, fulfilled was, neither more nor less. But Kabila's demands and extravagances exceeded what was dealt with, although he never indulged in his luxuries, and this irritated him greatly.

On 16 January 2001, Kabila was assassinated and had his death announced by Dominique Sakombi to the Congolese people on the national broadcast. In his place took over his son: Joseph Kabila, who remained in power until 2019.

In 2001, the world watched in perplexity on television the attacks that took place in the United States of America on 11 September. The world would never be the same again, especially the most important airports in major capitals. International surveillance of financial movements changed; not to mention the evolution of telecommunication technology, in which Enigma Enterprise had influence and of which thousands of human beings knew nothing.

My business relationship with Cosa Nostra was a pact that pleased Don Antonino. The participation in the business brought him financial benefits which made me a man of confidence, even in Vatican affairs, which few others had achieved. To this day we meet to deal with various matters, mainly business and politics.

My faithful African friends: Babu and Akin! They followed my advice and both of them moved to Tanzania. With part of the capital, they had at their disposal, they opened a company to serve tourists from all over the world. They first obtained their helicopter pilot's licences and in the first year bought two Robson 44 models and, with the growth of the business, two Bell 206s. Who accompanied them to Tanzania was Mabetu, who did not qualify in the medical examination as a pilot. The reason? I did not ask. They worked together discreetly and wisely.

I had the pleasure of visiting them in July 2019, not as a tourist, as a friend. Babu cried like a child on seeing me. Unfortunately, I have always been cold-blooded, yet I knew that the demonstration was coming from the heart of a man loyal to me. The place where we met was at Babu's farm, which was fully wooded and very well cared for. I was introduced to his wife and grown-up children and, to my surprise, two grandchildren.

Babu's eldest son, whose name was Mikimba, in honour of the mechanic, killed at the time of the missions when he heard his father call me "*Captain*", his eyes black as night shone, and he asked me without thinking: "Well? Are you Captain, sir? The eagle that flew over the African savannah? My father told of his adventures."

I looked at Babu and then at Mikimba and replied: "Don't believe everything he told you, because he certainly exaggerated every detail."

I realised at that moment that I could have been found out by Babu's recklessness. And from my lips, a cynical smile appeared once again, like so many others when in Zaire.

Are there ghosts? Yes, those we carry in our consciences, but Babu was one of my faithful African friends, the life he built in Tanzania brought him joy and happiness with his family, whom he showed respect and love. The next day, we gathered under a leafy tree and sat at the table for breakfast. Babu's children were disciplined and only began to serve themselves when their mother allowed them to.

One of them, about nine years old, asked me: "Are you a friend of my father?"

I replied to the boy: "Yes, I think so. Didn't you ask him?"

Babu's son looked at his father, remained silent after a few seconds and said: "My father said you are a good man. Are you a good man?"

And like a flash, my mind found the face of Enrico, the Italian, whom I killed without mercy. I replied to the boy: "I'm not as good as your father is."

Akin, besides being an excellent cook and mechanic, had skills as a pilot. He acquired a smaller property compared to Babu's. He lived comfortably with his wife and two children. When I saw him after so many years, he had not changed at all, just a few grey hairs, but his voice took me back in time when we used to talk over the VHF radios between the communications tower and the aircraft in contact: those are times that will never come back. He committed an unforgivable dare with me that day, as he invited me for a panoramic helicopter flight, knowing that

I did not like rotary wings. However, I accepted the ride, and it was wonderful to see him flying the Bell 206.

In the evening, after dinner, Babu and I sat in wooden rocking chairs on a wide veranda with a running board floor, while the children played on the swings he had built. In the sky a moonlight that only the African savannah has. Babu's farm was large and well fenced to avoid dangerous wild animals, especially for the children.

The temperate breeze in the air made the place very pleasant. He and I kept a silence that was only broken by the children's talking and laughing. His wife approached with a tray with a pot of coffee, lumps of sugar, small spoons and medium porcelain cups. Babu had a lovely family. He was kind enough to serve me coffee and handed the cup into my hands, then served himself. Silence accompanied us when he said: "Tomorrow morning we are going for a walk to a special place."

I replied: "Very well, I'll be ready."

Babu's Bell 206 helicopter was refuelled after breakfast. He came in on the right side and sat down; I sat on the opposite side since he was the commander on that flight. In helicopters, the 'commander's side is the right side. Babu's passion has always been for helicopters and flying them satisfaction that was mirrored in the African's shining eyes.

During the flight, he showed incredible places of impressive exuberance. Babu chose a meadow with abundant grass, not too tall, and landed. I followed Babu along a path that, surprisingly, led us to the source of the Nile River at Lake Victoria. It was a beautiful spot. He stood with his back to me and knelt. He took some water between his palms and drank it. At that moment I could kill him. Still kneeling, he turned his face to look at me and said, "Captain, I'm ready to die," and turned his face forward, his gaze on the horizon, while silence once again occupied our souls.

I looked at Babu, my faithful African friend, and held his right arm and said: "Stand up my good friend. I cannot do you any harm, much less take your life, for it does not belong to me. There is no reason for such cruelty."

He knew he had broken the "pact of silence" signed in 1997 by telling the adventures of a man known as Captain. That was a mistake I should not forgive; such is the code of true mercenaries. However, what would his death bring? Pain to a beautiful family, who would never forgive me. It is in those moments that we realise what the meaning of life is.

Babu stood up sobbing from crying, like a child, but my cold blood was imperative and persistent. I looked into the eyes of my faithful African friend with the same look that always accompanied me on the African savannah and said: "We should go back, otherwise Akin's lunch will go cold. Don't you think?"

I returned to old London two days later and to this day I keep in touch with both of them, with my faithful African friends. Babu never dared to tell what happened at the source of the River Nile at Lake Victoria.

Curiously, I learned that Tousset was killed during a fight in one of the bars on the outskirts of the city of Kinshasa when he openly defended the dictator Mobutu.

My secretary, Miss Elizabeth, on seeing me enter the office after returning from my trip to Africa, came with her traditional notepad and asked: "Did you have a nice trip?"

I replied: "Yes, the place was amazing. What's in your notebook? It looks urgent."

Miss Elizabeth said: "There is a man who insists on talking to you. He calls you Captain, his accent sounds Arabic, and he always talks about Allah." She sounded nervous because a person speaking in Arabic on the phone would make any one worried because of the prejudices created by the constants terrorist attacks.

I reassured her and said: "He is an old friend. Call him. His name is Iranian, in which case call him: *Mister Iranian.*"

My diary was busy, with several items pending, but nothing urgent. Miss Elizabeth booked a table at the Ritz Hotel, located at 150 Piccadilly, St. James, to have lunch at the restaurant at one p.m. next Friday with the Iranian. My driver Gregory arrived at the hotel at the appointed time. I was known to the restaurant's maître d', and he was kind enough to reserve a table for four people, as far away from prying ears as possible, even though there were only two of us having lunch. The maître's pocket received at least a hundred pounds sterling as a thank you.

I kept in touch with the Iranian all the time, but he never called my office, as our communication was by mobile phone. My Iranian "friend" walked into the restaurant and started making allusions to Allah. I did not mind his comments about his god, but they were unnecessary. He was still dressed in gold and precious stones, but no diamonds.

The ritual services of these restaurants are similar to so many others, what differs is exactly the price and the currency in which it is charged. After a few protocols, we started to talk about business. And what exactly did he want? Believe me! To open an air cargo company to work on millionaire contracts in the Middle East: Arab countries, among other places. The Iranian became a billionaire with me during missions in Africa and with the cover-up of several dictatorial governments. He wanted my immediate answer. I replied: "I think it is possible, give me a week."

The Iranian said: "If it were anyone else I would not give a day, but I have always trusted you. May Allah, the Great Allah, bless you Always."

I didn't mind paying the restaurant bill, the tip and for the goodwill of the maître d'. I left the Ritz Hotel and went to my office. I asked one of my lawyers to come to my office, tasked him with surveying the lives of the names contained on a piece of paper and demanded the four-day deadline on an emergency basis.

The contracts for the flight operations that the Iranian wanted required modern aircraft. The market was crammed with various models to choose from, among those stockpiled in deserts and airports. For such an operation I suggested the: B757-300ER. In four days, I had on my desk the complete folders of each name. I opened them one by one and read them carefully.

One of the reports that caught my attention was that of Jean-Pierre, which indicated that he resided in a boarding house, in financial difficulties due to gambling debts. Just like his brother, Jean-Batiste, who lost all his capital with loans never recovered, something incomprehensible but real. There I understood once and for all the scene I had witnessed at the Café de Flores in Paris a year ago, seeing him almost like a beggar. My eyes filled with tears. Do not confuse kindness with fragility; in me, there was kindness, but never the fragility of the defeated and losers.

Douglas resided in a rented house in Scotland and sometimes could not afford the heating. Joseph Marcos bought a hotel that came to bankruptcy with bank debts, resulting in the joint being repossessed by the bloody bank. And it didn't stop there. I read the report regarding Lee, who spent it all on prostitutes and gambling, to the point where he was considered scum among bookmakers.

Some of my men had exhausted their fortunes and were broke: financially and morally. I made a bold decision together with my team. The first action was to summon them to London with a reservation on a commercial flight, private rooms in a hotel, barber, full and adequate wardrobe, because I didn't want them to feel humiliated, especially the broke ones.

I didn't waste any time. I phoned the Iranian and said: "I will accept your request for help, and it will be on my terms and as I decide. Are we clear?"

He replied: "Understood. May Allah help us."

My men on leaving Rabat in August 1997 were on their own and with fortunes guaranteed, but not every human being is cut out to handle a lot of money. That is not to say that others did not achieve a stable life. I found that those who had a stable life lived it without a taste of emotion, like the German brothers, Kruger and Kauffman. They maintained a car rental company that did not prosper due to predatory competition from the giants of the rent-a-car market and were on the verge of closing down to save the company and some money.

Within a week, after being assured that everyone would attend the meeting, my men started arriving in London. My "*Legion of Misfits*" landed in the British capital. Each of them was met and taken to the hotel where they only confirmed their identity and received their room key. They were accompanied to a haircut, a tailor to measure and adjust their suits, as well as trying on top-of-the-line shoes. They didn't know who was paying for all the respect and comfort that surrounded them. They were given a schedule with times and with the saying: "Don't be late."

On the stipulated date and time, my men made their way to the business centre of the hotel. As they arrived, they noticed with surprise the reunion between old mercenary friends, men of honour and unparalleled loyalty.

My team provided security personnel to avoid any kind of inconvenience. When everyone was seated, one of the team members requested silence. And, without any kind of fuss, he announced that the lights would be turned off to show a short film. I "spied" the reactions. The film started with the name in French: "*Les Mercenaires*". This was followed by exclusive footage of the take-offs and landings of the aircraft we used during those years, which were obtained at great cost and kept with me all those post-Zaire years.

The silence of my men was glaring. The sound of the B707 and DC8 engines during take-offs, the unmistakable black curtains of the JT3-D engine discharge on final approach for landing, the noise of the JT8 engines of the B737-200 Adv and our favourite and unquestionable Hercules, which protected us from being killed during endless missions.

When the film ended, the lights came on. I entered with firm steps and stood face to face with my men once again. I confess that for the first time I trembled; not with fear, but with emotion, when I saw them and heard their name: *Captain*.

There was no reason to keep our distance, even if my security guards had recommended caution: I knew each of them, not as inveterate gamblers, indebted and broke, but as men who had faced the African savannah and the dangers that few can describe. That meeting was not a "personality cult"; far from deifying, we got down to business. I proposed a job as a commercial airline cargo pilot with a decent salary and warned them that the owner would be Iranian and I would be the administrator of the company, who would not fly with them. There was no protest about the "old Iranian" and my absence as a pilot.

Finally, I communicated that the intended equipment for

cargo flight operations would be the B757-300ER. One hundred per cent of those present agreed, and a new phase of their lives began, with the dignity they all deserved. After signing the work contract, they would undergo medical examinations and a ground school for the B757 in the United States of America. They knew how to fly, they were unbeatable eagles, but now they were to absorb a new doctrine, reality and posture, as true commercial airline pilots.

While my men were in London, another part of my team cleared everyone's debts, regardless of motives. It bought houses for the families of those in hardship and need, plus they received monthly and proportional aid while the pilot prepared for the B757. The aid was non-refundable. There were three months of intense training. What did you think? A pilot's life is not easy. The negotiation of three B757 freighters for purchase was quick and successful. Payment for the aircraft came through the Iranian's billion-dollar bank account, plus two more B757s as leases and with a preferential purchase option.

The main base of operations was assigned to the capital of a very wealthy country in the Arab region. From there it started to operate the flights of the millionaire cargo and postal contracts, with enviable results. A first-class hangar was bought with all the maintenance, loading and unloading facilities, including a large cargo yard. Everything was billed to the Iranian's bank account, as I only "work" with money from those interested in the business. I'm not a loan bank. I receive ten per cent of the monthly gross turnover from the contracts to run the company. "You can't leave a fox in the henhouse." Don't you think?

After a year of regular flight operations, I visited my men; I found them happy and purposeful in life. What they know best is to fly, no longer as mercenaries, but as legitimate world commercial aviation men. But, in their blood always runs the

221

"soul of the mercenary". Make no mistake!

When the Iranian learned that my "Legion of Misfits" was back in business, he almost had a heart attack. As I had made it clear that it would be my way, I would deal the cards, and preferably with my deck of marked cards. If you enter a "game" to lose, stay out of it and leave it to those who understand cheating. After all, "the world is a deck of marked cards", too bad you always get the worst cards of the marked deck. This deck was not made by me, because God exists, and none of us is Him. Remember?

The diamonds? Those kept in South Africa, of course you want to know where they went. I still keep a good part of them, I'll not reveal how much. The other part is in earrings, rings and necklaces of women all over the world, among lovers or not of extremely rich men, owners of oil wells, among so many other "profitable activities".

These diamonds are bought on a market that is difficult to access and secretive. Politicians and the royalty of some nations make a point of having them as "investments", for the purity quality of the diamonds and without fiscal note, paid for by the infinite laundering of corrupt money. Remember that: "The King is tax-hungry and loves to track your financial life." There are no angels in business.

To endorse the quality of these diamonds, the Belgique Minèire certified them with the "discovery of a new deposit" and offered a full guarantee, because a guarantee certificate has a different price, it is the diamond's identity card. Who takes care of these important details are the two sons of my Jewish accountant. Why men? I answer. Women don't have friends. They see the others as "potential competitors" and cultivate something dangerous: envy because they also want a diamond; and if possible without paying for it. I love women, preferably naked on the bed.

My accountant's sons are bright boys like diamonds, and my accountant is an old friend, who is now Rabbi of his religious community, and whom I hope will remain so. I know that once a year he goes to Jerusalem, Israel, to pray at the Wailing Wall, as well as taking care of some business of my interest. After all, he is a Rabbi, and with all the credit. You can believe it!

By the way, I could not fail to tell you that, unfortunately, in February 2019 in the city of Antwerp, the safety of a powerful bank was "opened" and from it, the customers' private boxes, containing jewellery of inestimable commercial value, were subtracted. The place in the city where this event took place is known as: "Diamond Quarter", where casually another similar event took place in 2003, called: "The theft of the century": they estimated the commercial value at one hundred million US dollars.

The clients should not worry in the first place, they pay high sums for the custody in the bank, since the jewels were kept under the custody of the bank; in the second place, every bank that dares to keep this type of "investment" has significant insurance that guarantees the payment of the goods kept, provided that, the good is declared by the client to the bank, otherwise, it'll be difficult to prove the property and the value of the jewel kept. Unless, when purchasing the jewellery, the client did not demand proof of payment and certification of the jewellery. For what reason did you not do so? How do you acquire such jewellery? I leave the conclusions to you. Remember: there are no naïve people in business, whatever it may be. There is a dose of intelligence, astuteness and audacity that few have the ability to perceive in a world as fast-paced as today's.

Who am I? What is my nationality? What is my origin? What does it matter? I can be right next to you, in a café in Florence or

Paris; at the train station in London, boarding at some airport to New York; watching a Juventus match, drinking a cappuccino or coffee. You will never know that a cold, calculating mercenary has prowled up close to you and that behind my dark pilot's glasses there is a pair of light brown eyes watching you.

What's my next move? Take over all the Iranian's contracts and the air cargo company. And you can bet that will happen soon.

"It's nothing personal, it's just business."

The End.